# Up from the Bend

Howard L. Katz

# Copyright

*Cover Design by Howard L. Katz*
*Copyright © 2012 by Howard L. Katz*

ISBN 978-0-9858575-0-9

Published July 8, 2012, by

**COBRA PRESS**
35125 Calle Nopal
Temecula, CA 92592
1-909-227-0202

*Cover and internal design © 2012 Cobra Press*
*All Rights Reserved.*

*Up from the Bend* is a work of fiction. All characters, names, cities and towns towns, and locations in this work are fictitious, except for Murphyville, Marfa, and Sanderson, Texas, and Trinidad, Colorado. Incidents described herein are the product of the author's imagination or are used fictitiously. Any resemblance to actual persons, living or dead, businesses, companies, events, or locales is entirely coincidental.

**For Kathy, Heather, and Travis**

# Up from the Bend

## Howard L. Katz

# Contents

# 1

A spectacular red, orange, and gold west Texas sunset bathed the front porch of the Bar CS ranch house. The house had been made for a single man, box shaped, with a main room, kitchen, bedroom, and an office where the business of the ranch was conducted. The house had also been decorated for a single man, only a few pieces of essential furniture sitting on bare wood floors.

The owner of the Bar CS, Charles Stockett, and his foreman, Ed Vargas, sat relaxing on the porch after having just finished a casual dinner of beef and beans, bread and butter, and coffee. Both men were dressed in soiled boots, work pants, and shirts, though their hands and faces were clean. Neither man wore a gun belt or had a long gun close by. Over glasses of whiskey, their conversation first focused on their day's activities, running the ranch and caring for their cattle, then moved on.

Charles said, "We've been harvestin' and grazin' off so much prairie grass here in the Big Bend the grass is mostly gone. What hasn't been trampled and killed at its roots doesn't get a chance to mature and go to seed before its eaten back to the ground. The grass don't have a chance of comin' back."

Ed replied, "There used to be so much grass, I thought there'd be enough to keep all our horses and cows fat forever. Seems I was wrong. I remember years ago in the Spring, the grass'd reach up the a cow's belly and well over a horse's hocks."

"Yes, I remember that. I remember, too, harvestin' it in early summer and storing it in the barns for winter. There was more'n we could use."

"I don't see we can do nothin' to bring it back 'less'n we stop runnin' cattle."

"I been thinkin' 'bout this for quite a spell. I think we've three choices," Charles answered. "The first is to take over ranches to the north that have fresher range and spread out the herd, but we'd use up that range in a couple a years. The second is to sell the ranch and move the herd north until we find good range and stop and settle. We'd go north from Murphyville through west Texas into the New Mexico Territory and maybe even all the way into Colorado. There's plenty of good grass and water along the way and we'd be sure to find a place that'd suit us. Many years ago, I was on a drive that took that route. Going from Murphyville all the way to Denver City, Colorado, with a herd our size could take two, three months. It's a good 600 miles and we'd be lucky to average ten miles a day. The third is to sell the ranch and the herd and start fresh somewhere else, doing somethin' else."

"The second seems best to me. I don't want to start fresh doin' somethin' else."

"Neither'd I. I want to keep ranchin'. I think I can sell the ranch to the Shunt brothers. They've been after me to sell for years. They'd probably not pay what I think its worth, but it'd cover our trail expenses and leave us enough to buy land and start anew."

Ed replied, "If you can sell and we can move, I'm in and I think most of our hands'd be, too. I'm ready for a change and the herd needs better range as soon as we can make it happen."

Charles thought about that for a while, then continued, "Alright. I'll go see the Shunt brothers tomorrow. You concentrate on the move, horses, equipment, supplies, and men. We'll need trail equipment and supplies and a full trail crew. We'll need a remuda of at least five horses for each of the riding crew, two US Calvary Escort Wagons to carry our equipment and supplies with two four-horse teams for each, a chuck wagon with two two-horse teams, and a good wrangler. It'll be like moving a small city."

"I'll put together the list of trail equipment and supplies. For crew, I'll start by asking our hands 'bout making the drive. We'll need all of 'em and then some."

"Find out who of our hands can handle a gun, Colt or Winchester, and can hit what they shoot at. While I'm seein' to the Shunt brothers tomorrow, you go to Murphyville and put the word out we're looking for experienced trail hands who can shoot. Five, if you can find 'em. We'll be going through some bad country and could run into rustlers, thieves, or Indians. Find time to stop by the mercantile and the assayer and buy maps of the country between here and Colorado."

Ed nodded he understood.

Charles refilled their glasses with whiskey and they sat engaged in their own thoughts about the move for well over a half hour. Together they stood, Charles went into the ranch house and Ed stepped off the porch and walked to the bunkhouse.

The following morning, after giving the hands their work assignments, Charles and Ed went to the barn and picked out saddle horses. Charles selected his favorite, a big-boned paint, and Ed took a sleek, well muscled bay. They curried their horses, cleaned and checked their feet, and tacked up. They stuffed a change of clothes in their saddle bags and tied them on their saddles behind the cantles. They slid Winchesters in their scabbards, tied canteens around their saddle horns and warm coats wrapped inside rain slickers over their saddle bags.

When they finished readying their horses, Charles said, "Plan to be back Wednesday, the day after tomorrow, by late afternoon and have dinner with me at the ranch house. Be careful."

They nodded to each other as they mounted. Charles left for the Shunt ranch to the northeast of the Bar CS and Ed left for Murphyville to the southwest.

# 2

Ed pushed his horse into a jog trot and kept that gait all the way to Murphyville, stopping only a few times to let his horse drink and blow. He made it to the Murphyville livery stable by early afternoon. He tied his horse to the hitching rail in front of the barn, took his Winchester, canteen, slicker wrapped coat, and saddle bags off his saddle, and the tack off his horse. He put his tack, saddle, saddle pad, breast collar, cinch, and bridle on the end of the hitching rail then rubbed his horse down with a handful of straw and put him in a stall in the barn with a liberal armful of hay and a bucket of water. Lastly, he moved his tack into the barn.

Ed picked up his Winchester, canteen, slicker wrapped coat, and saddle bags and carried them to the Murphyville Hotel and Rooming House where he took a room for two nights. In his room, he stood his Winchester against the wall, hung his canteen on the back of the straight-backed wooden chair, and put his saddle bags on the bureau. He unwrapped his coat from his slicker, threw the slicker to the floor in the corner of the room, put the coat on the bed as a pillow, and laid on the bed to rest. When he woke, about three hours later, he freshened up, left the hotel, and walked to Brewster's Saloon as twilight approached.

Brewster's Saloon wasn't much to look at from the outside. The building was made from unpainted boards, some straight, some twisted and warped. The high, false front was the only part of the building with any paint on it, **Brewster's Saloon** was displayed in bright red script over a white oval background. The painted area looked bright, cheerful, and inviting in comparison to the ugly, weathered building.

Ed entered through the batwing doors and stopped until his eyes adjusted to the light from the coal oil lanterns hanging from the chandeliers. He looked around the single large room. There were eight tables, six in front of the bar and two to the rear. Four of the tables in front of the bar were occupied by men drinking, eating, and playing cards, the other two were empty. The two tables to the rear were occupied by a few men drinking and negotiating with a half dozen whores. Along the side wall ran an ornate wooden bar with a row of bottles and glasses on shelves behind it. Several men stood along the bar drinking. Most were either ranchers or trail hands, the others appeared to be store keepers from their clothes.

Ed walked over to the bar and ordered dinner and a bottle of whiskey from the bartender. He took the bottle and a glass to one of the empty tables, sat, and looked over the crowd, assessing each patron as a possible Bar CS trail hand. At one table, there were seven men playing poker. Five of them appeared to be trail hands. They were wearing well used boots with spurs, riding pants, work shirts, vests, and gun belts. The other two were evidently gamblers, wearing well traveled, wrinkled suits. The bartender delivered Ed's his dinner. He ate slowly, and drank as he watched the game.

About a half hour later as Ed was finishing his dinner, one of the trail hands raised his voice and threw his cards across the table. The cards fell to the table in front of one of the gamblers, who stood up slowly from his seat, picked up the thrown cards, and threw them back at the trail hand, hitting him in the face. The trail hand jumped out of his seat, drew his Colt, and shot the gambler once, square in the center of his chest. The gambler fell backwards to the floor and didn't move. He was certainly dead before he hit the floor.

The shooter looked at the second gambler and said, "You got anything to add?"

The second gambler sat very still, both hands unmoving, palms down on the table, and replied, "No."

The shooter looked from one to the next of the four trail hands at the table, then around the rest of the saloon. He continued, "Anyone else got anything to add?" No-one met his gaze or replied, so the shooter holstered his Colt and sat back down at the table, raking in the money that had been in the poker pot as he sat. The four other trail hands and the gambler sitting at the table didn't move or say a word.

Ed thought the shooter might be the type of hand he was looking for, so he stood up from his table and walked over and hesitated behind the empty chair at the poker table. He looked directly at the shooter and said, "May I join you?"

The shooter nodded his approval.

Ed sat, nodded at the other trail hands and said to the gambler, "You'd better go. I want to talk to these men." The gambler stood, pocketed the money in front of him, and left the table.

Ed continued, "I'm looking for five hands to complete a trail drive crew. We're leaving this area within a month, going north, maybe all the way into Colorado. The five hands I'm looking for have to know how to shoot, both a Colt and a Winchester, herd cattle, and able to scout trail ahead of a herd. We'll be going through some rough country and may run into trouble. And most of all, they gotta be loyal to the brand. Are you the men I'm looking for?"

The shooter said, "Name's Harold. These other four are Lefty, Bob, Snake, and John. The five of us may be interested. We can do all you're looking for and we're loyal to the brand we work for. We don't shy from hard work or gun play. If the pay is right we may go with you. Meet us here tomorrow night and buy us dinner. We'll tell you then."

Ed nodded, stood, and returned to his table.

Ed returned from Murphyville on Wednesday in the early afternoon. He removed his Winchester, canteen, slicker wrapped coat, and saddle bags from his saddle. He removed his tack, then brushed his horse and turned him loose in the corral to stretch and roll.

He checked with the hands about what had happened while he was away. Nothing out of the ordinary was reported to him. He cleaned up from the trip and dressed for dinner in clean work clothes.

# 3

Charles kept his horse at a walk for the first half hour to thoroughly warm him up. He stopped to let the horse rest and get a mouthful of grass then squeezed him forward into a gentle lope and kept him in a lope for the next hour when he stopped again to let the horse blow and rest. When he felt the horse had had sufficient rest, he picked up the horse's head and pushed him back into a gentle lope. After an hour, when he was close to the Shunt ranch, he checked his horse into a trot then a walk to cool him out.

When Charles reached the Shunt ranch, he rode through the front gate and up to the main house, dismounted, and tied the horse to the hitching rack. After he tied his horse, he looked at the house from one end to the other. The house was amazing. It was southern colonial-style sitting on a raised foundation, freshly painted white, two-stories, with wide, covered porches on both the ground and second floors, and had white, fluted columns holding up the second story porch.

Jeffrey Shunt, the older brother, came out of the house and greeted him, "Charles, what a surprise. I'm so glad you came to visit. I hope your visit is good news. It's late in the day, I hope you'll be able to stay for dinner and spend the night with us."

Charles replied, "Yes, of course, I'd planned to stay, and thank you for the dinner invitation. Though, I have to return home tomorrow."

"Good. Leave your horse and your things. I'll have the houseboy bring your things to the guest room and one of my hands attend to your horse. Please come in and let's have a drink. James is inside, I'm sure he'll be as pleased to see you as I."

They walked up the stairs to the porch, entered the house through the front door, and continued to the parlor. Jeffrey motioned Charles to sit on a plush velvet couch as he went to the sideboard and poured three glasses of whiskey from a cut crystal decanter.

James Shunt entered the parlor just then and said, "Jeffrey, Charles. It's nice to see a neighbor come calling."

Jeffrey handed Charles and James their glasses and the two Shunt brothers sat across from Charles in hard backed, wooden chairs.

The three of them sat quietly for a minute, sipping their whiskey. The Shunt brothers were waiting for Charles to tell them why he was there, too polite to ask.

Charles finally took the initiative, "Jeffrey, James, you've been asking me for several years to sell my ranch to you. I've decided to sell and move my herd north. If you're still wantin' my ranch, now's your opportunity. Make me an offer."

Jeffrey looked at James and said to Charles, "You've taken us by surprise. We're not ready at this minute to make you an offer. But, if you'll allow us time to confer between now and dinner, over dinner we'll be prepared to discuss a purchase with you."

"That'll be fine, I'd like some time to rest and clean up. Keep one thing in mind, you'll be buying only the ranch, not the brand, nor the herd."

Charles returned to the Bar CS late Wednesday afternoon. He took care of his horse and tack, bathed, and dressed for dinner in a clean work pants and a white shirt.

# 4

Charles and Ed met on the porch of the Bar CS ranch house at sunset late Wednesday afternoon. The sky was again a spectacular red, orange, and gold.

Charles asked, "Whiskey?"

Ed replied, "Yes, please."

Charles poured and said, "Hope you've got somethin' to tell me."

"Yes, quite a lot, actually. What d'ya want to hear first?"

"Crew. Which of our current hands are comin' with us?"

Ed said, "I questioned all our hands about the drive. 15 will come with us, three won't. Of the 15, 13 will stay with us where we settle, two say they'll want to return here to west Texas. Of the 15, only six have a handgun or a rifle or both. Those six claim they can hit what they aim at."

"OK. What about your trip to Murphyville. Did you find anyone to come with us?"

"Yes. I found five trail hands in Murphyville willin' to make the drive. I met 'em at Brewster's Saloon. I was lookin' 'em over when one of 'em outdrew and killed a gambler over a poker hand. They say they're loyal to the brand they work for and aren't afraid of hard work or gunplay. All five say they have both a Colt and a Winchester, know how to shoot, hit what they shoot at, and know how to herd cattle and scout trail. I don't know anythin' else 'bout 'em, but I hired 'em. They'll be here Friday."

"OK, that's great, but we'll have to watch 'em. How large is our crew and do we need anyone else?"

"With you and me, we'll have a crew of 22, 11 with the herd, two on each of the two escort wagons, two on the chuck wagon, a cook and his helper, two with the remuda, one of the new hands scouting trail, and you and me. I think we've got a full crew."

"Horses and wagons?"

"We've got two escort wagons and a chuck wagon. We've got two four-horse teams for each of the escort wagons and two two-horse teams for the chuck wagon. And, we've got enough ridin' horses, not quite five for each rider, better'n four, but that should be enough."

Ed stopped for a breath, and continued, "We'll need to do some maintenance and make some repairs to the three wagons, grease axles, check tongues and traces, and patch canvass covers. We'll have to take all the pots, pans, and utensils from the kitchens for cooking and the metal plates, cups, and flatware for eatin'."

Ed stopped again, thought a bit, and continued, "We'll sleep out on the drive except in bad weather, when we'll need tents. And, we'll need tents where we settle, since we probably won't have a main house or a bunkhouse anytime soon. We should have a large tent for storage, two medium sized tents, one for each of us, and two-man tents for the hands. That's ten two-man tents, but we should probably have three extras. That's 16 tents with poles and ropes, which'll fill one of the escort wagons."

"Good, see to it."

"The tents and initial trail supplies I'll round up in the next couple of weeks. I should be able to get what we don't already have in Murphyville. If we have to drive all the way into Colorado, we'll have to purchase more trail supplies on the way. We won't be able to carry enough for a three-month drive. We'll have to have money with us to purchase trail supplies along the way."

Ed stopped for another breath, and continued, "I bought a couple of maps. I've studied 'em so I'll leave 'em with you."

"Excellent," Charles replied. "I think you've covered everythin'. I'm sure you'll plug any holes before we leave. I'll be sure to have the money we'll need, but we mustn't spread the word we're carryin' a lot of money, especially with the new men you've hired."

Charles thought for a while and continued, "I was successful, too. The Shunt brothers will buy the ranch and 500 head of cattle. They gave me a partial payment yesterday and they'll give me the rest in a couple of weeks. We agreed they'll take ownership May first. They'll send a crew over before then to select and separate their 500 head. Since today is the second of April, we'll have to be gone in exactly four weeks, that's April 30. Start rounding up the herd and be ready to leave. If we go all the way to Colorado, we should get there 'bout the first of August."

"We'll be ready," Ed replied.

Charles concluded, "Since we're going north through west Texas, the eastern part of the Territory of New Mexico, and possibly all the way into Colorado, we'll take the Goodnight-Loving Trail, which follows that general route all the way to

Denver City. That's the route we followed when I was on a drive north several years ago. I'll confirm the exact route after I've had a chance to study the maps. I should be ready to discuss the trail in a couple of days."

Charles poured each of them another glass of whiskey. They drank, thinking about the trail drive ahead of them and their destination.

# 5

Three days later, Ed and Charles were having a simple breakfast on the Bar CS main house porch. Ed said to Charles, "I've finished puttin' together the list of hardware, tents, food, and cooking utensils we'll need to start the drive. I looked over the two escort wagons and the chuck wagon and put together a list of repairs we'll have to make to 'em and their harnesses, tongues, and traces. I'm going to Murphyville after we finish breakfast and purchase what supplies I can and drop off things to be repaired at the saddle maker and the blacksmith. I'll probably have to spend the night in Murphyville. If I can't get all of the supplies we need in Murphyville, I'll send a hand east to Sanderson on the train to purchase 'em and have 'em shipped to Sunrise. I'll hire the mercantile or the livery to gather up all our purchases and repaired items and bring 'em out to us here at the ranch. That'll save us the time and energy of going back and picking 'em up ourselves. I'm sure we'll have everythin' we need when we need it. That leaves us free to round up the herd and get ready to pack the wagons. Anythin' you want to add or change?"

Charles replied, "Can't think of anythin', but give me the list and I'll go over it right now and make any additions and changes I think necessary. Get another cup of coffee and give me a minute with the list."

Ed went into the house to the kitchen and poured himself another cup of coffee. He returned to the porch, sat at the table, and waited for Charles to finish reviewing the list.

Charles finished his review, looked up at Ed and said, "Your list is extensive and complete. I've nothing to add or change."

Ed nodded.

"If you have the time, I'd like to discuss our route."

"I have a little time before I have to leave for Murphyville."

"Good. How much do you know about the Goodnight-Loving Trail?"

"Only the name."

"You should know a little of the trail's history, so I'll tell you somethin' about it, if you don't mind?"

"Please do."

"The Goodnight-Loving Trail was one of the first of the post-war trails to be blazed across West Texas," Charles explained. "Charles Goodnight established a herd of cattle in the Keechi Valley of Palo Pinto County in the late 1850s and ranged his cattle across Palo Pinto, Parker, and Young counties.

"After servin' in the frontier militia during the war, Goodnight rounded up his cattle in the spring of 1866 and headed for the Rocky Mountain minin' region. To avoid Indians, he decided to use the old Butterfield stagecoach route to the southwest, follow the Pecos River upstream, and proceed northward to Colorado. This route was almost twice as long as the direct route, but it was much safer. You with me?"

"Yes."

"While buyin' supplies for this trip, Charles Goodnight encountered Oliver Loving, and the two decided to join forces. Their combined herd numbered 'bout 2,000 head when they left their camp 25 miles southwest of Belknap on June 6, 1866. Their route took 'em past Camp Cooper, by the ruins of old Fort Phantom Hill, through Buffalo Gap, past Chadbourne, and across the North Concho River. They crossed the Middle Concho and followed it west to the Llano Estacado, crossed New Mexico and proceeded to Denver City, Colorado. With this drive, the Goodnight-Loving Trail was born.

"Goodnight and Loving used this trail several more times before Loving was mortally wounded in an Indian attack in New Mexico in September 1869. Just before he died, Loving made Goodnight promise to see that he was buried in his hometown cemetery in Weatherford, Texas. Loving's remains were temporarily interred in New Mexico while Goodnight and his outfit completed the drive. Returning to New Mexico, Goodnight had his cowboys flatten out all the old oil cans they could find and solder them together to make a tin casket. Loving's remains were placed into a wooden coffin, which was put inside the tin casket. Powdered charcoal was packed between the coffin and the casket, and the metal lid was sealed. The whole contraption was crated and transported to Weatherford for burial."

Ed thought for a minute and said, "Seems to me that we aren't very close to the Goodnight-Loving Trail. How do we get to it?"

"We'll start out going northeast out of Murphyville followin' Paisano Creek to where it joins Musquiz Creek. We'll follow that continuin' northeast until it ends and then follow its headwaters until we get to Fort Stockton. We won't go into Fort Stockton, we'll circle it to the east, turnin' north to the Pecos River. We'll cross the Pecos, followin' it basically northward through the rest of West Texas and into the Territory of New

Mexico. When we get to Santa Rosa, New Mexico, we'll turn northeast, skirt the Ratón Mountains to the east, pass into Colorado, and turn west toward Trinidad."

Ed hesitated, thinking, and said, "Is there somewhere on that route you believe we could stop and settle?"

"There's different kinds of country and plenty of grass and water along that route. There's low and high plains with grass and scrub brush, and hills and mountains with scrub brush and forest. There's plenty of rivers and streams. We'll see lots of places to stop and settle. The problem will be findin' the one that'll feel right. We may have to go all the way to Trinidad to find it. It can't be directly on the trail. It'll have to be a valley a good distance off the trail, 'cause there'll be other drives on the trail after us and we don't want 'em comin' through our land, eating our grass, and minglin' with our herd."

"What 'bout weather?"

"All along the Goodnight-Loving trail the winters are cold and the summers are hot, though, the higher the elevation, the colder the winters and cooler the summers. We're goin' in late spring, early summer, so we won't experience the extremes, cold or hot. The climates shouldn't differ too much from here, some places five to ten degrees colder, other places five to ten degrees hotter."

"Charles, this has been really interesting and stuff I really need to know, but I've got to check on the hands and get to Murphyville. If it's alright with you, I'd like to continue this when I return."

Charles nodded his approval.

19

Ed stepped off the porch, walked to his small, one-room cabin, gathered the personal items he'd need for the trip to Murphville, and went to barn to collect the buckboard and a team of horses. He had a couple of hands load the items to be repaired into the buckboard's bed. After the buckboard was loaded, Ed climbed onto the seat. Tim, one of his hands, climbed onto the seat next to him, and they left for Murphyville.

They arrived in Murphyville in the middle of the afternoon. Their first stop was the blacksmith, where they dropped off items the blacksmith could repair and to order a box of assorted size horseshoes and a box horseshoe nails they'd need on the drive. Their second stop was the saddle maker, where they dropped off the collars and harnesses for the escort and chuck wagon teams that needed repair. Their third stop was the livery, where they dropped off the now empty buckboard and its two-horse team. They'd pick up the buckboard and team when they were ready to return to the Bar CS. They walked to their last stop, the mercantile.

They entered the mercantile and stood inside near the door waiting their turn to be helped. There were two women in front of them buying cloth, thread, and needles. Ed and Tim stood quietly, but looked around the inside of the mercantile noticing the shelves and tables containing canned goods, cloth, ready-made clothes, and boots out where customers could see them up close and handle them and the shelves of guns and ammunition behind the counter where they couldn't.. They also noticed the sacks of beans, flour, and sugar stacked on the floor.

When Bob, the owner of the mercantile, finished with the two women, he walked over to Ed and Tim, nodded at Tim and said to Ed, "Morning."

Ed replied, "Morning Bob. In case you didn't know, Charles Stockett sold his ranch to the Shunt brothers. We're movin' the brand, the cattle, and everythin' that isn't nailed down north in less than a month."

"Ed, I didn't know. Seems kind a sudden."

"Not really, Bob. Charles been thinkin' 'bout moving for some time. Seems like for him and me it's time to move on. I've got a list of stuff here I need for the drive, and I need the stuff soon as possible."

Ed handed the list to Bob, who slowly read it, read it a second, and a third time.

"Ed, this is a lot of stuff. I only have some of it now. I can have everything 'cept the tents within the week. For the tents you'll have to go to Sanderson."

"That's what I figured. Tim, here, will be on tomorrow morning's train to Sanderson to buy the tents and have them shipped here to you. I'd 'preciate it if you pick up our stuff from the blacksmith and the saddle maker in a couple of days. Stuff there is already paid for. After you receive the tents from Sanderson and have everything else together, I'd 'preciate it if you'd load it all on a wagon or two and bring it out to the Bar CS."

"Of course. The freight out to the Bar should be reasonable. You gonna pay now for everything you're buying from me today?"

"Yes, and we'll pay the freight when you deliver."

"That's fair enough. Let's go over to the counter and tally it up."

# 6

Ed returned to the Bar CS the middle of the next day. After leaving the buckboard and team with the wrangler, he checked with the hands. Finding everything in order, he went to his cabin, hung his Winchester on the gun rack, put his personal things on his bunk, washed, changed clothes, and went to the main house.

Ed found Charles sitting on the porch drinking water from a tall glass and reading a book. Charles looked up hearing someone climbing the steps to the porch, saw Ed, and said, "Afternoon, Ed. How'd it go?"

"Great. I dropped off everything needin' repair and ordered the supplies on the list you approved. I sent Tim on the train to Sanderson to order the tents, they weren't available in Murphyville. Tim will have the tents shipped to the Murphyville mercantile. Bob at the mercantile will put everything together, tents, stuff from the blacksmith, stuff from the saddle maker, and what we've ordered from him. He'll load it onto a couple a wagons, and send it out here in a week or two. We'll have to pay him for the freight when it's delivered, but he told me the freight would be reasonable. I've money left from what you give me."

"Good," said Charles, putting out his hand and accepting the small leather sack offered by Ed.

Ed said, "Charles, you know I've never been on a drive before. Though I don't think it can be too different from herdin' on the ranch."

"Ed, a trail drive is much different from herdin' on the ranch and my response to what you just said may be longer than my description of the Goodnight-Loving Trail. Are you ready to listen a while?"

"Yes."

"Stop me if you have any questions"

"Alright."

"A typical trail drive outfit consists of a trail boss, ten to 15 trail drivers, each with a string of horses, a wrangler or two, who drive, herd, and care for the horses, and a cook, who may have a helper. The trail boss may be the owner or someone hired by the owner to lead the drive. During the day, the trail drivers move and graze the cattle and at night keep the herd quietly bedded down. Ten or 12 miles is considered a good day's drive, though actual daily travel is controlled by the availability of grass and water and condition of the cattle. The object is to fatten the cattle along the way, or at least not to have them lose weight. Cattle don't trail in a group, they string out in a long line, though the line may be several head wide. Right off, several natural leaders usually make their way to the front of the line, or point as it's called, the others fall into an irregular line several head wide behind 'em. A herd the size of ours could stretch a couple of miles. With me so far?"

"Yes."

"In many ways the cook is the most important member of the drive and generally is paid better than any of the other hands, except, of course, the trail boss. The cook drives the chuck wagon ahead of the herd and selects stopovers for noonday meals and locations for evening meals and night campsites for the hands, the remuda, and the herd. Typical trail meals are beef or bison steaks, SOB stew, made from calf parts, chuck wagon chicken, really bacon, Pecos strawberries, or beans, sourdough bullets, or biscuits, and strong coffee.

"One or more scouts precede the herd looking for potential trouble, like Indians, rustlers, or a trail made impassable because of a ravine, a cliff, or a deep or fast flowing river. The best pair of hands ride 'point' at the front of the herd, pairs of hands ride 'flank' on the sides of the herd, the last flank pair is called the 'swing' riders, and several hands ride 'drag' at the back of the herd. For us, we'll have two scouts, two at point, eight at flank workin' in four pairs, one of each pair on opposite sides of the line, and two at drag. And, if you add the four hands on the escort wagons, the cook and his helper, and the two of us, we'll have a total crew of 22. Communication is by hand signals, adapted from Plains Indian sign language, or gestures with hats.

"Everyone shares the job of watching the herd at night, normally one or two hands at a time, hoping the cattle don't become spooked and begin running. If they run, they won't all go in the same direction and there's no telling how far they'll scatter. It could take days or even weeks to get them all together again, if ever they can be. Still with me?"

"Yes."

"Drives normally begin after the spring grass comes up. That's why we're leavin' now, to get the tail end of the spring grass. A trail herd of 2,500 to 3,000 is considered the most favorable size for long drives. Smaller herds require 'bout the same-size crew and the same costs, larger herds face watering and feeding problems and are generally unwieldy to handle. We've got 3,500 head now, but since we're selling 500 to the

Shunt brothers before we leave, we'll start on the trail with 3,000, the maximum favorably-sized herd.

"On the trail, bedrolls are carried rolled up and tied in the chuck wagon, thrown out in the evenin' and rolled up, tied, and loaded up again on the chuck wagon in the morning. When the weather is good, the crew sleeps in the open. We'll keep extra blankets in the chuck wagon for chilly nights. If the weather turns really cold or it rains or snows, we'll have to set up the tents.

"If there's room in one of the escort wagons, we'll have a calf wagon. That's where we'll put calves born on the drive, since they won't be able to keep up on the trial. Our hands will pick up the calves, put each in a separate sack, and put 'em in the calf wagon. At night, we'll turn the calves loose. Their mothers will find 'em and care for 'em overnight. In the morning we'll sacked 'em and throw 'em back in the calf wagon for the day's drive. If we don't have room for the calves, we'll eat 'em. Still with me?"

"Yes."

"On the first day of the drive, we'll make an early start in the morning and drive the herd at a fast walk all day. The purpose for making a hard drive the first day is to be as far away from the herd's home bedding ground as possible the first night. If a herd is too near home when bedding time arrives, the cattle'll try to return home and we'll lose control of 'em.

"After the first day, the pointers can allow the herd to slow down, spread out a little, and graze along the way, but the herd has to be kept headed up trail, always. If we want to move the herd faster than their grazing gait, we tighten 'em up, that is, reduce the spread between 'em and urge 'em forward. We'll wanna go faster if we have to get somewhere special for bedding or reach a watering hole. I think that's enough for now."

Charles stopped and watched Ed thinking his way through everything. He waited a few minutes and finally said, "That was an awful lot to take in, but remember, I've been up this trail before. The scouts you just hired are experienced trail hands and we've got other good hands to rely on. We're gonna be fine, so is the herd, and so'll you."

Ed reluctantly nodded.

"When we start out, I'll be trail boss. As you get used to the drive and I see you can take on more responsibility, I'll turn more of the job over to you 'till you've got it all, you're the trail boss. That alright?"

"Yes, Charles, that's fine. Thank you."

Charles closed the conversation with, "OK, Ed. You've got a lot to do between now and April 30. You say we'll be ready. You better start getting there. I want to leave as scheduled."

# 7

Sunrise, Colorado, is near the center of a large valley shaped like a shallow bowl. There were very few trees left in the bowl, most of those that had been there had been cut down for firewood, to make room for grazing cattle and horses, and for lumber to build stores and houses. The surrounding hills were still covered with pine forest. The valley floor slopes gently downward to the southern hills and gently upward to the northern hills. To the east and west, the valley floor is basically level, raising slightly toward the hills in both directions.

The Union Southern railroad and the road through Sunrise connect it to the south to Albuquerque in the New Mexico Territory and to the north to Denver City, Colorado. They both enter the valley from the south-south-west and leave to the north. To the north, the railroad and the road pass through the towns of Penance and Trinidad on their way to Denver City. Sunrise and Penance are in the very southern part of Las Animas County. Sunrise is just on the Colorado side of the border between Colorado and the New Mexico Territory. Penance is north, an hour by train or a couple hours by horse. Trinidad is further north, another two hours by train or four or five hours by horse. Trinidad is the county seat. A couple of miles north of Sunrise the road forks. The north track goes on to Penance. A few miles on the east track, the road forks again. The north track goes to the Sleeping L ranch and several ranches north of it. The east track goes east-north-east and eventually gets to Dodge City, Kansas.

On July 12, two days after we eliminated the Sunrise Police Chief, Aldus White, and his 25-man police force, nine of us were sitting around a table in the restaurant of the Chicago House Hotel and Saloon, the fanciest hotel and saloon in Sunrise. There were Rawlins Knight, County Deputy Sheriff from Trinidad, Colorado, Ward Layne, owner of the Chicago House Hotel and Saloon, Lowell Williams, owner of the Silver Chalet Saloon, and the six of us who had fought against White and his police force, Alexander Gadson, Bird Corre, Lacy Burnham, Dyson Lewis, Gregory Jackson, and me.

Alexander Gadson and I had been together as lawmen-for-hire for more'n 20 years in many towns from Colorado to Texas and back. In some of the towns, Alexander had been the marshal and I had been his deputy. In other towns, Alexander had provided security for one or more of the saloons and I had backed him up.

Bird Corre is a Mexican-Chiricahua Indian 'breed, our friend for years. His friendship started when he rescued Claire Knowles and her mother from a renegade Indian sometime back.

Lacy Burnham was a professional gunslinger hired by the late General Love to kill Alexander, but never had the chance because of the trouble with the Police Chief Aldus White and his policemen diverted his attention.

Dyson and Jackson are marshals from Penance, Colorado, a town north of Sunrise, midway to Trinidad. They've been our friends for years and have carried our water on more'n a few occasions.

The Chicago House saloon was a single large L-shaped room with a mahogany bar running from the front wall to the rear along the long wall. In the area at the foot of the 'L' were tables where private drinking and business was conducted, especially with the whores. The main part of the room was where card playing and hard drinking happened. Behind the bar were shelves holding bottles of liquor and glasses. Behind the bottles and glasses was a wide, tall mirror, which made the room look twice as large as it was.

There were two entries into the saloon, one from the boardwalk through batwing doors and the other from the restaurant. The restaurant was located between the hotel lobby and the saloon.

Ward and Lowell were dressed in their saloon-keepers best. Ward had on a gray suit with faint white stripes and a matching vest. Lowell was wearing a solid black suit with a matching vest. They both wore white shirts, string ties, and clean, polished black boots.

Alexander was wearing a trail-worn black suit, white shirt, fancy vest, and well-worn black boots with rowel spurs. I was wearing brown riding pants tucked into high top brown boots with rowel spurs, a brown shooting coat, brown vest, and an almost matching brown shirt.

Bird was wearing deer-skin pants with fringe along the outside seam running from his waist to where his pants entered the tops of his high-top, deer-skin moccasins and a deer-skin shirt. Though he was a breed, his dress, the way he wore his hair, his carriage, and the way he acted and usually spoke were completely Indian.

Dyson and Jackson were dressed similar to trail hands, work pants, work shirts, well-worn boots with spurs, and black cloth vests. There clothes didn't seem to change much. Else, they had several sets very similar to one another.

All of us were heeled, though Ward's and Lowell's pistols were out of sight under their coats in shoulder rigs, not displayed at their waists in gun belts, as were those carried by all the rest of us, except Bird. He carried a large Bowie knife. Its handle stuck prominently out of the top of his right boot. The same knife he'd used to slit his brother's throat when his brother and a group of crazed young bucks from the reservation tried to wipe out Sunrise a couple years ago.

Ward Layne had invited us to the Chicago House for a breakfast celebration commemorating the elimination of Police Chief Aldus White and his police force and to consider how to protect the town in the aftermath. We were alone in the restaurant; Ward had closed the restaurant to other patrons. He'd had a feast prepared for us. There was steak, eggs, potatoes, biscuits and butter, and plenty of coffee, served by two lovely waitresses. Conversation during the meal was light and impersonal.

After the waitresses finished clearing our breakfast dishes, Ward called Clay McCans, the Chicago House bartender, to bring us a bottle of whiskey and glasses, which he brought on a tray and set on the table. Ward picked up the bottle, poured a liberal glassful of whisky for each of us, and told Clay to bring another bottle.

Alexander began speaking to Knight loud enough to get everyone's attention. All other conversations stopped. Alexander said, "Rawlins, you got here right quick, the day after the shootin' stopped."

"I surely didn't want to get here the day before or the day of the fight, even if I'd a known it was goin' to happen. I would've had to choose sides and may've thrown in with White," said Knight with a smile. "News of the massacre was delivered to Trinidad by a passenger on yesterday morning's train. And, since you eliminated, that is killed or ran out a town, the complete Sunrise Police Department, I had to get here quickly to make sure there was just cause for what you done."

"Weren't a massacre. We was outnumbered almost four to one. We was only protecting ourselves and the citizens of Sunrise. You see it different?"

"No, don't. Was the right thing to do, getting rid of White. Law supposed to protect. White and his thugs were not only abusing their power, but collectin' protection money, too. White was as crooked as they come."

Ward said, "Getting rid of White and his thugs was good for the town. Our problem is what to do now? We got Alexander and Emmett protecting the Chicago House and the Silver Chalet, but we ain't got no law enforcement. Nobody's protectin' the town, the other businesses, the people."

Knight thought for a while, and replied, "Seems to me you got three choices. First, you can hire a town marshal and a couple of deputies. Second, you can hire a new police chief and a couple of policemen. Third, you can continue as is, no law enforcement. Though, I don't recommend that. If you hire the correct marshal and deputies or police chief and policemen to protect the town, you won't need Alexander and Emmett. If you don't hire law enforcement, you'll have to keep Alexander and

Emmett, but the town won't be protected. Seems to me, you don't have much of a choice."

Ward looked at Alexander and asked, "Alexander, what do you think we aught to do?"

We waited for Alexander's response. He seemed to be looking out the door, not listening to us or looking at anything in particular, but I knew he'd heard everything and had already decided what should be done.

"Ward," Alexander said, "seems to me that it ain't up to me and I shouldn't have a say in the decision."

"Alexander, we need your advice."

Alexander looked at Ward, then at Lowell, and finally said to me, "Emmett, you speak for us."

I said, "Well, I can speak for you and me, but if you're including Lacy and Bird in us, they'll have to speak for themselves."

Alexander nodded.

I collected my thoughts and continued, "Seems to me the town needs law enforcement. A new police chief and a couple of policemen wouldn't be accepted right kindly 'bout now after the town's experience with White. I think the town would accept a marshal and a couple of deputies, especially, if the townsfolk knew and trusted the new marshal and his deputies. Alexander would be the right marshal, with me and another deputy to back him." I turned in my chair, looked at Lacy, and said, "I think Lacy Burnham should be the second deputy. The townsfolk know him and know he chose the right side when the ball went up and we fought White."

Lacy was surprised by what I'd said. He looked at Alexander then at me for support, and receiving none, knew he'd have to speak for himself. He replied, "I'd like nothing better than to be Marshal Gadson's second deputy."

Ward said, "Now, 'bout Bird."

Everyone's attention shifted to Bird, but before Ward could continue, Alexander interrupted saying, "Bird and me have some private business to settle before he'll be able to answer."

Bird nodded, but didn't otherwise respond.

Everyone was quiet for a minute then Ward looked at Lowell and said, "Lowell, I think you'll agree with me to hire Alexander Gadson as town marshal and Emmett Masters and Lacy Burnham as his deputies, but you and me can't make this decision for the town by ourselves. We need to meet with and get the agreement of other town business owners and maybe some of the local ranchers, since all of us together will have to pay their salaries and expenses. And, we'll probably have to agree to their town rules, again. We should form a town council that has the authority to appoint new leadership for the City Commission and elect a mayor, too."

Lowell replied, "OK, but law enforcement, a town marshal and two deputies, gotta come first. Leadership of the City Commission and election of a mayor are not as important and can wait. We should personally consult the other town business owners and send riders out to the local ranchers to hear from them."

Everyone at the table agreed. Glasses were refilled and emptied one last time. We all thanked Ward for breakfast, then all of us except Ward and Lowell stood and walked out of the Chicago House, leaving the two of them talking quietly.

We stood in a small circle in the middle of Main Street. Gregory Jackson glanced at Dyson then said to Alexander, "Eliminating White and his thugs was fun. I'm glad Dyson and me were able to help and I'm glad we all came through it standing, but it's time for us to get back to Penance. I'm sure they sorely miss us or maybe they've replaced us by now. We'll be leaving on the morning train. On down the road, Alexander."

"'preciate what you done for us," Alexander said. "I won't forget."

Dyson and Jackson each nodded at Alexander then at me, Lacy, and Bird, turned toward the livery, and walked away.

Knight said to Alexander, "I got to see the sheriff and make sure he understands what happened here and that there's no reason to bring any of you in for murder. I'll be leaving on the morning train, too." Knight nodded at Alexander then at me, Lacy, and Bird, and followed after Dyson and Jackson.

Alexander did not reply to Knight, but to us he said, "There's something important Bird and me need to discuss, but since the four of us are close, Lacy and Emmett, you two should be part of our talk. Whyn't we walk to my house and sit a spell."

# 8

We walked to Alexander's house, each of us absorbed in his own thoughts. Alexander had the house built the first time we'd lived in Sunrise. It was a fairly large house on a raised foundation at the end of Main Street. The house had a covered porch, kitchen, parlor with a brick fireplace shared with the kitchen, and two bedrooms, all with wood floors. The outside was overlapped wood boards, starting at the bottom for waterproofing. The roof was wood shake.

When we arrived at the house, we climbed the steps to the porch. There were only three chairs. Alexander, Lacy, and I sat, Bird remained standing. He positioned himself so he could see the street and us at the same time.

Ella and Claire came out onto the porch with a jug for us and two glasses for themselves. Lacy and I got up and gave the women our chairs. I took the jug from Ella and poured whiskey in the women's glasses, took a drink from the jug, and passed it to Lacy. We sat quietly, enjoying our whiskey as it warmed us from the inside out on its way down our throats. We stared out at Main Street, delighting in the light afternoon breeze.

After some time of silence, Alexander looked at Bird and Claire, got up from his chair, and said, "Before the ball went up and the shootin' started between White and us, General Love said I was to inherit the Sleeping L if anythin' happened to him. He said that to a bunch of us outside Sunrise before the first shots were fired. As you know, General Love was killed and the Sleeping L and everythin' on it is now mine. Problem is, I ain't no rancher, and at this point, don't wanna be. Don't want the ranch, neither. I been thinkin', the Sleeping L best be worked by a man and his wife who'd put down roots and give the ranch stability. I'm givin' the ranch and most everythin' on it to you, Bird and Claire, if you'll have it and work it. I've some money left from Marfa and I'm gettin' more from the General's estate. I can loan you enough to keep the ranch runnin' until it can pay for itself. You can pay me back when you're able."

That was the longest speech I'd ever heard Alexander make.

I wasn't surprised at what Alexander said because he told me sometime back he intended to do it, but the others were shocked still and quiet. Ella's mouth was open and moving. She looked sort a like a fish trying to breath out a water. She was trying to speak but couldn't. Bird and Claire sat stunned, looking at each other, but they seemed to decide without speaking they'd accept Alexander's offer. Claire jumped out of her chair, ran to Alexander, threw her arms around him, buried her face in his chest, and began to cry.

Bird looked at Alexander and said, "Blue-eyed devil crazy, but we accept."

Alexander smiled at Bird and turned to me and said, "Emmett, whyn't you and Lacy go out to the Sleepin' L tomorrow and fetch that handsome two-bench surrey and the team of grays so the ladies, Bird, and me can visit our ranch in comfort and style. Lacy'd better go with you 'cause he used to work for the General and they know him. Be sure to take your eight-gauge."

== < > ==

Lacy and I left Sunrise for the Sleeping L the next morning on the road north, just after sunrise. At the first fork we took the track east toward Kansas. At the second fork, we took the track north toward the ranches. After about an hour, we turned off the north track onto a wagon track toward the east and crested the hill just west of the Sleeping L. We saw the gray leopard appaloosa stallion and his mares in the middle of their meadow. The mares' heads were down grazing and they didn't pay us any mind. The stallion was very aware of us, standing between us and his mares at full alert with his head and tail up. He glanced excitedly first at his mares then at us, snorting and stomping his front hooves. We circled them at a distance along the rim of the meadow. When we reached the other side, we dropped down from the rim to the ranch.

John Fields, the Sleeping L ranch foreman, met us as we rode up to the front of the main house. Several of his ranch hands stood a ways behind him. Not one of them wore a gun belt or held a Winchester. Lacy and I were heeled, each of us had a Winchester in a saddle scabbard, and I was holding my eight-gauge across the pommel of my saddle. We appeared to be expecting trouble, we had taken Clausewitz's advice, you got to prepare for what your enemy can do, not what you think he might do.

"Morning Emmett, Lacy," Fields said rather coldly. "Somethin' I can do for you?"

"Mornin', John," I said. "Yes, there is. Alexander asked us to come get that handsome two-bench surrey with the matched team of grays so he can bring Ella, Claire, and Bird out here to visit his ranch. Have someone hitch 'em up. I'll drive it back to town."

He started to protest, but I raised my hand to stop him and said, "You know the General said that Alexander was to get the ranch if anythin' happened to him. He said that in front of a group of us as witnesses. That makes Alexander owner of the Sleepin' L and everythin' on it. I suggest you start followin' Alexander's orders and honor his requests as you did the General's. I'm sure when Alexander gets here tomorrow you and him will have lots to discuss about the ranch and how he wants it run."

I let that sink in a minute, then continued, "Lacy and I will be inside the main house. Bring the surrey here when it's ready and come get us."

He bristled at the instructions, but didn't say anything. He gave me a hard stare then turned and walked head down toward the barn.

Lacy and I watered our horses at the trough in front of the main house and tied them by their reins to the hitching rail. We climbed the stairs to the porch, knocked on the front door, and without waiting, went inside directly to the parlor.

The Mexican houseboy came running into the parlor excited that his house was being invaded. I know he had been with the general for several years, but he still dressed in what seemed to be Mexican peasant clothing. He looked a bit out of place, but comfortable. I said to him, "Alexander Gadson is the new owner of the Sleepin' L. You are to follow my instructions as you would his or those of General Love. Now, bring us that decanter of good whisky and glasses."

He also bristled at the instructions, but didn't say anything. He left the parlor at a fast shuffle and quickly returned with a full decanter of whisky and two glasses. He poured us generous portions of whiskey and left the room. I leaned my eight-gauge against the wall and Lacy and I sat comfortably at the table in the center of the room, sipping the General's good whiskey, waiting for the surrey.

Fields announced his arrival at the main house door with a loud knock. Without opening the door, he called out loud enough that we could hear him clearly inside, "The surrey's ready and waitin'."

I took the almost full decanter of whisky as a present for Alexander, picked up my eight-gauge, and Lacy and I exited the house through the front door. Fields was standing with the surrey keeping the team still and quiet. We stopped at the edge of the porch and looked at the surrey.

I said, "Thank you, John, for readyin' the surrey so quickly. We'll be back tomorrow with Alexander, Ella, Claire, and Bird. Probably be 'bout midday."

We took the bridles off our horses and put on halters with lead ropes attached in their place. We tied our horses to the back of the surrey with the lead ropes and climbed onto the front bench. I took up and snapped the reins, clucked to the team, and we left for town at a trot.

About an hour out from the ranch we realized we was both hungry. I stopped the surrey, Lacy got down, went back to our horses, and retrieved our lunch from our saddlebags and grabbed the canteens looped over our saddle horns. He returned to the surrey and I clucked to the team to move 'em on. We ate in the surrey while we continued on towards Sunrise, letting the team loaf along. When we finished eating, I pushed the team back into a trot.

The rest of our trip was uneventful. When we arrived at the livery late in the afternoon, I said to the stableman, "Unhitch the team. Give 'em each a good rubdown, an inside stall, a bucket of fresh water, and some hay and grain. I believe Alexander will want 'em and the surrey to have permanent homes here. Hitch the team back up early in the morning, we'll need the surrey ready right after breakfast."

Lacy and I put our own saddle horses away, walked across the street together, and went our separate ways. I knew Lacy would go to the Café Madrid for dinner, go to his room at the Chicago House, and get to bed early.

I went straight to the Chicago House. I needed to tell Alexander about the day and what I had arranged for the following morning. I was sure he was sitting on the front porch of the Chicago House waiting quietly for something to happen at one of the saloons he and I were hired to protect. With the falling evening, it was time for me to make the first nighttime tour of the saloons.

I didn't see Alexander outside the Chicago House. So, I went through the batwing doors to look inside.

# 9

I stood just inside the batwing doors of the Chicago House saloon and let my eyes adjust to the dim light from the coal oil lanterns attached to the chandeliers. Looking around the room, I saw Ward and Alexander sitting together at one of the two tables near the back. They were alone at the table. The other table was occupied by three men and three whores whooping it up and having a grand time. I went to join Ward and Alexander. As I passed Clay standing behind the bar, he handed me a clean, empty glass that I filled when I sat down with Ward and Alexander.

Ward looked very upset and flustered, even his clothes were more rumpled than usual. He nodded at me and said to us, "Sabrina White paid me a visit this afternoon. She told me she'd run a couple of cribs in New Orleans before she married Aldus and they moved here." We knew about Sabrina's past and continued looking at Ward without commenting or changing expression.

"Sabrina wants to run my whores, set their prices, and send 'em clients, her clients. She don't want my whores spending time with anyone unless they've been sent by her. She wants a percentage of everythin', of all the take of the Chicago House, liquor, whores, hotel, restaurant, everythin'. And, she wants her percentage without buyin' in."

"She should pay dearly for a percentage of the Chicago House." said Alexander. "She should have money. Aldus collected a lot for protection and stole a lot over the last three years."

"No, she don't think she needs to buy in," said Ward. "She thinks just bein' known as my partner would bring me so much additional business it would be a good investment for me to give her a percentage free."

"Thinks a lot of herself," said Alexander.

"Wonder if she's worth it?" I replied.

"Said to me she was," said Ward.

"Then she must be," said Alexander. "Don't think she'd say anythin' that ain't true. Emmett, you'll have to try her and see whether she measures up to her boasts before Ward here makes a deal."

"No, not me," I said. "Bein' with Jewel Marion now and again is enough for me. Besides, Jewel'd be jealous if I spent time with Sabrina and may do somethin' stupid. Can't let that happen."

"No, can't," Alexander said to me. Then turning to Ward he said, "Ward, as schemin' and dishonest as Sabrina and Aldus were, I'd be very careful of any dealin's with her. People hold bad feelin's about Aldus 'cause of how he treated 'em. People may turn again' you if she's known as your partner. They'll want, ah, retrition. Emmett?"

"Retribution, Alexander," I said. "Meaning, punishment considered to be morally right and fully deserved."

"Yes, take retribution for her and Aldus' actions out on you," finished Alexander. "But, as she says, having her as your partner could be good for business, she's pretty and dresses well. You've got to give this serious thought. Come back and talk with us after you've thought 'bout it some more, but I'd recommend you tell her you're not interested and see what she does after that."

Ward sat quietly for a bit then stood up from the table and walked toward the front of the saloon greeting customers as he went.

Alexander and I were still sitting at the table, sipping whiskey. Alexander said, "Emmett, you know Ella set considerable store by Sabrina, how upstandin' a community member and church goin' lady she was and how she had made a new life for herself after bein' a whore in New Orleans. This happens, could cause Ella considerable confusion."

"Alexander," I said, "we'll just have to wait for Ward's decision. You advised against this partnership, but, as usual, we'll have to await developments."

I stood up, adding, "Alexander, I'm going to the Silver Chalet. Make sure there's some whisky left in that bottle when I get back."

I went through the batwing doors out onto the boardwalk in front of the Chicago House and stopped. I waited for my eyes to adjust to the dark before walking down the stairs to the street. I stayed on the street walking slowly all the way to the Silver Chalet where I climbed onto the boardwalk and entered through the batwing doors. I hesitated just inside the doors to let my eyes adjust to the dim light coming from the coal oil lanterns hanging from the chandeliers and scanned the room.

The Silver Chalet Saloon was a perfect saloon, only second to the Chicago House Hotel and Saloon as the fanciest place in Sunrise. The saloon was a single large square room with an oak bar running from the front wall to the rear on the wall to the left of the batwing doors as you entered. Behind the bar were shelves holding bottles of liquor and glasses. Behind the bottles and glasses is a wide, tall mirror, which makes the room look larger than it really is. Tables were distributed such that the room was divided in two. Toward the front of the room were six tables where card playing and hard drinking happened. Toward the rear were four tables, three together and one in the far corner. The whores and their clients partied at the three tables. The fourth was reserved for Lowell Williams, the owner. There were two entries into the saloon. One was off the street through batwing doors. The other was from the hotel.

The saloon was mostly full, several men were standing at the bar, four of the six tables had four or more men drinking or playing cards, one table in the rear had two men and two whores drinking and preparing for action, and another table in the rear had three available whores waiting for prospects.

The men standing at the bar seemed contented and friendly. So did the men at the tables, except for two men at the table closest to me who seemed agitated. They began shouting, stood, kicked their chairs back, and glared at each other.

Before I could bring my eight-gauge up level and say anything to them, they drew pistols from shoulder holsters and fired simultaneously. It sounded like a canon shot booming across the saloon, deafening. Both men fell to the floor and didn't move.

I said in a loud voice, "Don't nobody move. Who were these fellas and what caused this?"

One of the men at their table said, "They's drummers, or were. They arrived on this mornin's train. Supposed to leave tomorrow mornin' for Trinidad. Don't know their names, but they surely didn't like each other. Been at each other kind of quietly for the last hour or so."

"They was heeled," I said. "Everyone here knows the rules. How were they able to have pistols on 'em?"

Lowell Williams, owner of the Silver Chalet, was behind the bar. He was wearing suit pants, a white shirt and string tie, and a long white apron. He looked to be the perfect bartender. I said to him, "Lowell, didn't you check to see if they was heeled?"

He answered, "Emmett, I asked 'em personal, but they said they wasn't. Their pistols were in shoulder rigs under their coats, I didn't see 'em."

I replied, "OK, Lowell, you can only do so much without pattin' 'em down. Get this cleaned up and have their bodies taken out of here. Have someone find out where they were stayin', collect their personals, and have them delivered to the marshal's office in the mornin'."

Lowell nodded at me and said, "They had rooms here." He turned to two of his workers standing at the end of the bar and said, "Boys, get to it, do as the deputy says."

Lowell turned back to me and said, "Emmett, go over to my table and sit for a spell, I need to talk to ya."

I nodded and went to Lowell's table and sat. Lowell reached behind the bar, retrieved a bottle of whiskey and two glasses, and came to his table and sat across from me.

He said, "Sabrina White came here this mornin'. She told me she'd had cribs in New Orleans before she married Aldus and come here."

I nodded.

"She wants to take over my whores, set their prices, and send clients here to the Silver Chalet, her clients. And, she wants a percentage of everything, whores, liquor, food, and rooms. She wants to be my partner in the Silver Chalet."

"What is she offerin' for this partnership and percentage of the take?"

"She won't pay anythin'. She thinks bein' my partner would be such a big draw the additional business would more than offset what she should pay for a percentage."

"Did you agree to anythin'?"

"No. I told her I'd think about it for a while and get back to her. She said I could have a week."

"Lowell, Sabrina went to the Chicago House after she visited you and made the same demand of Ward. His answer was the same as yours, he'd have to think 'bout it and get back to her. Ward asked Alexander and me what we thought of her offer and Alexander advised against acceptin' it and to wait and see what she does. But, now that she's made the same offer to both of you, somethin' bigger is on her mind, like getting a piece of all the saloons. I think you should talk with Ward before you consider this any further and don't do anythin' until you talk with Alexander."

Lowell took a sip of whisky and sat quietly for a while. He finally stood up, nodded to me, and walked back behind the bar greeting customers as he went.

I stood, took one last look around the Silver Chalet and walked through the batwing doors to the street. I stopped on the boardwalk before walking down the stairs to the street waiting for my eyes to adjust to the dark. As I waited, I thought fondly about Jewel Scarlet and thought it would be a good night to pay her a visit.

# 10

The Café Madrid was owned and run by a Spanish family, a man, Sebastian Gomez, his wife, and their two children. The man waited table and did the heavy carrying and cleaning. The wife did the cooking and light cleaning. The children washed the dishes and made food ready for cooking, cut up vegetables, gathered eggs, cut up meat.

The Café Madrid had two rooms. Clients entered from the boardwalk into the main room at the front. It held five tables. Two of the tables were round and three were square. The larger of the two round tables was in the middle of the room. There were six chairs around it. The smaller of the round tables was toward the back of the room. There were five chairs around it. The three square tables were along the walls facing the street. One side of each of the square tables was against a wall and there were three chairs at each of the tables, one on each open side. The second room, at the back, was the kitchen. There were two entries into the kitchen, one from the main room and the other to the street to the rear, where the food, water, and wood fuel for the stoves was brought in and the slop was taken out. The Café Madrid opened for business at sunrise. They had to get there long before sunrise to be ready for customers by then.

Lacy, Bird, and I met Alexander, Ella, and Claire at the Café Madrid for breakfast about one-half hour after sunrise. We ordered coffee from the Spaniard, who said he now had six chickens, and, lucky for us, had six eggs that morning. The two women each ordered a biscuit and an egg. The four of us men each ordered biscuits, an egg, and fried sow belly.

The Spaniard brought cups and poured coffee. Our feelings about the coffee at the Café Madrid hadn't changed. It was the second worst in Sunrise. The worst was Ella's, but we'd never tell her.

The Spaniard brought the women their breakfasts first. Our breakfasts came a few minutes later.

As we ate, the conversation turned to our visit to the Sleeping L. Alexander said, "Bird, you and Claire are taking on a big responsibility with the ranch. You'll be fightin' an uphill battle, being that you're a breed and Claire's a woman. Emmett, Tell 'em what they're gonna be up against."

I looked at Alexander, astonished that he'd bring this up. But as I thought about it, in my gut I agreed this had to be discussed before it was announced at the ranch, to the other ranchers, and here in town that Bird and Claire were taking over the Sleeping L.

So, I said, "Bird, people aren't gonna take to a breed ownin' the largest and best ranch in these parts. Not only don't they like Mexicans much, but they sure don't like Indians. They put up with you 'cause of what you did for the town when your brother tried to destroy it and 'cause you're our friend, but as a ranch owner, they may not be as acceptin'. They may even be hostile."

Bird looked thoughtfully at me and said, "I can handle this."

I continued, "And, you, Claire, people here 'bouts think a woman should be a wife or a whore, not part owner of a ranch. People may not take kindly to you as the wife of a breed, especially a Mexican one. And, they may not accept you tellin' 'em what to do."

Claire looked at each of us in turn for a couple of seconds ending with Bird. She smiled at Bird and said, "We can handle this."

"OK, then," Alexander said. "There's a couple things need to be settled about the ranch. The first is a new name, and you, Bird, should be ready to tell John Fields, the ranch foreman, the new name soon after we start talking with him. The Sleepin' L was a fittin' name for General Love, seein' as his last name began with an 'L'. It don't fit you."

Bird looked at Claire and said, "Sleeping L fits Claire."

Alexander continued, "A ranch's name associates the owner with his ranch, and most people look to a man as the owner. That way, when the ranch's name is spoken the owner comes to mind. If you keep the name Sleepin' L, people will continue to associate the ranch with General Love not with Bird Corre, Claire Knowles, or the two of you together."

Claire shook her head quickly left, right, left rapidly and said, "Bird."

Bird smiled and said, "My Mexican name is Pajarito Corre, from the Chiricahua, Little Bird Running. Chiquita want Bird part of the ranch name. We could name the ranch with my Chiricahua name reversed, Running Little Bird, or just Running Bird."

Claire smiled and nodded her head in agreement.

Alexander said, "Very good, that's settled. Bird, the next thing to decide is who'll be the ranch foreman. John Fields has done a good job. He's honest, hard working, the hands respect him, he's respected by the other ranchers, and he's respected here in town. I recommend you keep him as foreman."

Bird thought for a while, then said, "I also respect John Fields. I know he's done well at the Sleepin' L. We'll keep him on until we get settled and see if things continue to run as well with us there."

Alexander continued, "As I said when I asked you and Claire if you wanted the Sleepin' L, Ella and me want a few things from the ranch for ourselves. Bird, Claire, is that alright with you?"

"Yes," Bird replied. Claire nodded her agreement.

"Ella, you and me need to walk through the main house and decide what few things we want after the business part of our visit is over. Our place is small, so we can't take much. To start, I've got my sights set on the buggy and the team of grays."

Bird and Claire nodded in agreement.

"Last thing before we go is to agree who runs the ranch. Bird, Claire, I've given the ranch to you. You own it. It's yours to run. You're in charge of everything that happens there now. You don't have to listen to me or Emmett, even though we'll offer you as much advice as you need, probably more'n you'll want. You can put in your effort and build it up or you can squander your time and loose it. Understand?"

"Yes," Bird replied. Claire again nodded her agreement.

"Remember," I added, "the four of us here at this table love you and consider you our kin. We'll gladly give you our time and all the help and advice you need and want."

Lacy, Alexander, and Ella nodded their agreement.

Alexander said, "Bird, you should be prepared to start talkin' with John Fields as the owner of the Running Bird, the person in charge, the person with authority. You're not his friend, he works for you, you're his boss. And you, Claire, you need to be prepared to be the mistress of the house and tell the houseboy what you want and what he's to do. You're not his friend, you're his boss. You should be friendly with all the other hands in the same manner."

Bird and Claire both nodded in response.

Alexander paid for breakfast. He turned to me and said, "Emmett, be sure to bring your eight-gauge."

We rose from the table and left the Café Madrid heading for the livery. Alexander, Ella, Bird, and Claire waited by the hitching rail in front of the barn while Lacy and I went into the barn to collect and tack up our horses. When our horses were ready, we walked them out of the barn, mounted up, and rode to where the stableman was standing with the buggy talking with Alexander. The team of grays was fully hitched and standing quietly.

The stableman said to Alexander, "This is a really good team. They're quiet and respectful. It's nice to have 'em here. And, I've got a good place inside at the back of the barn to store your buggy out of the weather."

"Thank you," said Alexander. "The team will stay here with you, there isn't a better place for 'em in Sunrise. Since I got no other place to store the buggy, it'll have to stay here with you, too. I 'preciate you've got a place for it inside."

Alexander turned to Ella, Bird, and Claire and said, "Time to go. Ella, I'll drive. You and I'll sit on the front bench."

Alexander helped Ella climb up onto the front bench and climbed up next to her. When Alexander and Ella were settled, Bird helped Claire up onto the back bench, and climbed up next to her.

Alexander snapped the reins and started the team with a cluck, moving them out of the livery yard turning right onto Main Street. Lacy and I followed a short distance behind.

As we passed out of town and headed onto the road to Penance and Trinidad, Alexander picked up the pace to a jog trot.

# 11

We left Sunrise going north on the road to Penance. The road was two parallel, shallow wagon-wheel ruts with a wide raised flat area in between them. The road rose steadily toward the hills. At the fork a couple of miles out of town, we took the east track leading toward Dodge City, Kansas.

We kept a leisurely pace, trotting some and walking some, passing out of the valley into the hills. We trotted some to eat miles and walked some to rest the horses. We stopped every so often to let the horses blow. We let our saddle horses and the surrey team drink at some of the clear, fast running streams. A couple of the streams had steep banks. At these, we filled a bucket and watered the team from it, first one horse then the other. We stopped at midmorning to give the horses a longer rest and allow us to dismount and stretch our legs. When the horses breathing was back to normal, Alexander, Ella, Bird, and Claire climbed back into the surrey and Lacy and I mounted back up and we continued on our way.

I had a canteen full of water hung over our saddle horn from which I occasionally drank. Water is the best thing to drink on a hot day. Drinking whiskey while riding in the sun gives you a terrible headache.

A little further on we crested a hill and looked into the small meadow where we usually saw the appaloosa stallion and his mares. We weren't disappointed. They were there, seemingly waiting for us.

As usual, the mares had their heads down grazing and didn't pay us no mind. The stallion was standing between us and his mares at full alert with his head and tail up. He was glancing excitedly between his mares and us, daring us to go after his mares and watching to make sure his mares didn't try to leave. We circled them along the crest of the hills surrounding the meadow, finally reached the other side, and dropped down off the hills to the ranch.

When we arrived at the ranch house, we were met by the foreman, John Fields, and several of his hands. All of them recognized Alexander, Lacy, and me. We were greeted respectfully, but not enthusiastically.

Alexander said to Fields, "Mornin', John."

"Mornin', Alexander."

"Whyn't you get the rest of the hands and the houseboy. I want to introduce these others to everyone," indicating Ella, Claire, and Bird. Fields nodded and went off the fetch them.

We all stood quietly waiting for Fields to return. When he was back with the rest of the hands, Alexander continued, "I want to introduce these three people to you. First is Mrs. Stella Penn, next is Miss Claire Knowles, and last is Mr. Pajarito Corre. Mrs. Penn is with me and is my companion. The other two, Miss Knowles and Mr. Corre, are very good friends of mine. Mr. Corre was instrumental in defeatin' the Indians who nearly destroyed Sunrise a while back. In fact, Mr. Corre killed his own brother who was leadin' the attackin' Indians."

Alexander stopped for moment, then continued. "'bout an hour before General Love was killed in the gun battle in Sunrise between us and the Sunrise Police Department a week or so ago, he told a group of us that he'd sworn as witnesses, that when he passed, this ranch'd be mine. The witnesses to that testament were Emmett Masters, Lacy Burnham, Pajarito Corre, Dyson Lewis, Gregory Jackson, and me. I've decided to pass ownership of this ranch on to Mr. Corre and Miss Knowles. They now each own a one-half share of this ranch."

Alexander stopped and waited a minute letting that sink in, then continued, "They've decided the Sleepin' L shall be known from now on as the Runnin' Bird. They'll be moving into the main house and they'll be runnin' the ranch from now on. I don't want to hear 'bout any trouble between any of you and Mr. Corre or Miss Knowles. If there's any trouble, those causin' the trouble will answer to me. You got questions or objections, I want to hear 'em now."

Alexander looked straight into the eyes of the closest hand, held his attention for a second, moved his gaze to the next hand and the next until he had looked directly at each of the assembled hands. There was no response from any of them.

Alexander said, "Alright. That's all I've got to say."

Bird stepped forward and said, "We are truly happy to join you here at the Runnin' Bird and hope to continue the successful operation of the ranch. Claire and I would like all of you to stay with us. We think this ranch has great promise and a great future for all of us to share. Those of you who don't want to stay step forward."

Bird waited for anyone to step forward, no-one did. He continued, "Thank you for staying, and especially you, John. You'll continue as foreman. And, the rest of you, I appreciate all you've done here in the past and hope to get to know each and every one of you very soon. Please come introduce yourselves to me and Miss Claire when you can. That's all for now. Return to your assignments."

As the hands were leaving, Bird turned to Fields and said, "John, please join me in the house and we can continue with the details." Bird motioned to the houseboy to come close and said, "Take Miss Knowles with you into the kitchen and help her make lunch for the six of us and Mr. Fields."

We six, John Fields, and the houseboy went into the house. Claire and the houseboy went into the kitchen to prepare lunch. Bird and Fields went into the parlor and began talking in earnest about running the ranch. Alexander, Ella, Lacy, and I got a decanter of the General's whiskey and glasses and returned to the porch to sit, sip, and wait for lunch.

We'd just sipped our glasses dry when Claire came onto the porch and said, "Lunch is ready."

We followed her into the dining room just as the houseboy was finishing filling water glasses from another decanter. The General surely had a bunch of them.

Claire pointed at the houseboy and said, "José."

We guessed that he had told her his name or she was making one up for him. Either way, the name José stuck.

The table was set for seven and lunch was already on the table. We sat, Bird at the head, and started serving ourselves, passing full platters of food.

Bird said, "Claire, you and José, made a great lunch, especially in such a short time."

Claire bowed her head, smiled, and blushed.

When we'd finished lunch and the conversation about the ranch and events in Sunrise was winding down, Bird said to Fields, "Select two hands to go through the house with Alexander and Ella. They'll carry the things Alexander and Ella choose outside to the porch. When Alexander and Ella are finished, have the team of grays hitched to the surrey and have a team hitched to a buckboard. Have the stuff Alexander and Ella chose loaded onto the buckboard. Claire and I will return to the ranch tomorrow with our stuff and the buckboard."

Fields went outside and selected two hands who returned with him. Fields introduced the two hands to Alexander and Ella and left the house to have the surrey and buckboard made ready. The two hands followed Alexander and Ella out of the room.

A little while later, the two hands started carrying stuff out of the house to the porch. First came two smaller dressers. The kind usually placed on either side of a bed as nightstands. Then came two small coal oil hurricane lamps for the nightstands. And, last came a box of kitchen stuff with a cut crystal decanter full of whiskey perched on top.

Alexander and Ella came back into the parlor. Alexander motioned to me they were through. So, Lacy and I left the house to tack up our horses and make ready to leave.

When Lacy and I had finished readying our horses, we led them to the house and tied them by their reins to the hitching rack. When the surrey and the buckboard were ready and the stuff Alexander and Ella had chosen was loaded and secured on the buckboard, Alexander and Ella climbed up onto the front bench of the surrey, Bird and Claire climbed up onto the bench of the buckboard, Lacy and I mounted our horses, and we left for

Sunrise, the surrey first so Alexander could set the pace, followed by the buckboard. Lacy and I rode drag.

# 12

We arrived back in Sunrise late in the afternoon. We went straight to Alexander's and Ella's house to unload the buckboard. First, I carefully lifted the whiskey-filled decanter from the box of kitchen utensils and set it on the porch table for safety. They we began in earnest unloading the rest of the stuff and putting it on the porch away from the front door, the two small dressers, two small coal oil lamps, and the box of kitchen utensils. Ella and Claire stayed at the house to put things away. They would probably rearrange everything already in the bedroom to accommodate the two small dressers.

We four men went on to the livery to brush, feed, water, and put up the horses, clean and hang our tack, and stow the surrey and buckboard and their harnesses. Then, we went to the Chicago House for dinner. We decided earlier not to tempt Ella to cook for us tonight. We were too tired for surprises.

While we were eating, Ward Layne and Lowell Williams came to our table. Ward was carrying a bottle of whisky and two glasses. Lowell was carrying four more glasses.

Ward said, "Evening, Alexander, Emmett, Lacy, Bird," as he looked at each of us in turn. He returned his focus to Alexander and said, "Glad to find you here tonight. May we join you?"

Nodding at the two empty chairs, Alexander replied, "Ward, Lowell, anyone bringing a bottle of whisky and glasses to our table is surely welcome."

Ward smiled and said, "This morning while you were out of town we met at City Hall, several of the town's business and property owners and some of the local ranchers. We formed a town council and elected five councilmen. Lowell and I are two. I was selected council chairman and Lowell treasurer."

"Congratulations, Mr. Mayor." I said.

Ward continued, "Thank you, but the council chairman is not the mayor. An election for mayor will come later. All men in the town and local ranchers will be entitled to vote in the election. However, now that we have a town council, we have a local government and the council chairman is the closest thing we have to a mayor."

Ward stopped to breathe, then continued, "The first thing the council agreed upon was to hire a town marshal and two deputies. Taking your advice, Emmett, we decided to offer the marshal's job to you, Alexander, and the deputy's jobs to you, Emmett and Lacy. If we need a third deputy sometime in the future, Alexander, you'll have the freedom to choose him. Bird, we have a job for you, too. We want you to be our town tracker and be available when we need you. We certainly hope the four of you'll accept."

Alexander thought for a minute and answered, "I think I can speak for the four of us. We accept your offer, with some conditions: first, the pays gotta be right; second, the town's gotta pay our expenses; third, you agree to the town rules we had when we was marshalling here before; and fourth, we have the use of the old marshal's office as the jail and what was White's police department offices in City Hall as the marshal's office."

Ward looked to Lowell for support, Lowell nodded his head, and Ward replied, "I'll do the best I can to respond to your conditions. First, pay. The council approved $200 a month for law enforcement paid for by a tax on each of the town's businesses, the local ranchers, and small contributions from all people living in Sunrise. We agreed to pay the marshal $60 a month and each of the deputies $45 a month. Combined, the marshal and the deputies'll receive $150 of the $200. Pay'll be disbursed by the town council treasurer on the first of the month. Your jobs start immediately and so'll your pay. Is that acceptable?"

Lacy and I looked at each other then at Alexander, all three of us nodding our approval. Alexander said to Ward, "Accepted."

Ward continued, "Second, expense money. The other $50 a month is for expenses, ammunition, livery, posse, tracker, and prisoners and their keep. You'll pay Bird $1.50 a day from the expense money when he's working. If you need a posse, you can pay each of 'em $0.50 a day from the expense money, but Bird and posse members pay their own expenses. And, you'll buy prisoners' meals from the Chicago House or the Silver Chalet. Expense money will be disbursed by the town council treasurer as you need it. Agreed?"

We looked at Alexander and nodded our agreement. Alexander said, "Agreed."

Ward continued, "Third, your town rules. Your old town rules worked for the town before, but the town has grown and things have changed. We can start with your old town rules, but the town council will make changes to 'em by enacting laws to replace 'em, of course with your help and agreement, Alexander. You and your deputies will be responsible to enforce those old rules still in effect and the new laws as they're passed."

Alexander answered, "Agreed, as long as the rules and laws make our jobs easier and protect everyone. But if the old rules and new laws conflict, we'll be at a crossroads."

Ward said, "Last, the offices. The new offices in City Hall don't have a jail, so you'll have to use the old marshal's office as the jail and the new offices for marshalling business. I think that covers all of your conditions."

Ward waited for Alexander to respond. Alexander, Lacy, Bird, and I looked at one another and nodded our agreement. Alexander said, "We'll have to reckon with the rules and laws as time passes, but as it stands, you just hired a marshal, two deputies, and a tracker."

Ward refilled our glasses and we drank to seal the agreement.

When we stood to leave, Ward motioned to Alexander and me to step aside. He came close to us and said quietly, "Sabrina come to see me this morning. She told me she didn't want to partner with me and Lowell after all. She's decided to open her own place, a gentlemen's club, initially at her house. Said she'd expand her house or move into larger quarters when necessary."

Alexander replied, "Good. You and Lowell aren't gonna be involved with her. Less to do with Sabrina the better."

"Yes," I said, "but we'll need to watch Ella. She looked up to Sabrina. If Sabrina's successful, Ella might go visiting. That could change your home life."

Alexander didn't say anything, but I could tell he was thinking about it.

We walked through the batwing doors out onto the boardwalk in front of the Chicago House. Bird nodded at us and quiet as a ghost disappeared into the night. Alexander, Lacy, and I strode down the stairs from the boardwalk into the street on our way to make our first official town rounds since becoming marshal and his deputies.

Alexander said, "Our rules ain't gonna be good enough very long. They're gonna want their own laws. That'll change things."

I replied, "As Ward said, the town has grown and things have changed. The question is, can we change with 'em?"

Alexander was quiet as we walked, and finally said, "Don't know if we can or if we'll have to. Gotta await developments."

# 13

Charles Stockett and Ed Vargas had seen several likely places to stop and settle along the way north from Murphyville through west Texas, the Territory of New Mexico, and into Colorado, but they had not found the perfect one. They were looking for a valley with low hills surrounding a large grass meadow with scattered mature trees and a wide, free-flowing, shallow river running through the middle of it.

At midmorning on the first of August, exactly 90 days after leaving Murphyville, they were riding point, leading their herd west. They had crossed the state line into Colorado five days ago, continued north for two days, and turned west. Now, three days later, they crested a low hill and looked down into a nearly round valley, maybe 10 miles across.

Charles motioned to Ed to break free of the herd, move to the right, and let it pass them. Standing just over the crest of the hill looking down into the valley, Charles took a spyglass out of his right saddlebag, slid it open, and slowly looked around the valley. What he saw was exactly what they had been looking for. He stopped sweeping the valley and focused on the valley's north side. He saw the log cabins, corrals, and pole barns of what appeared to be three small ranches, less than a mile or so apart, where the hills rose gently up from the valley floor. Not one of the ranches was fenced or had a major structure.

Ed said, "This is the valley we've been looking for."

Charles replied, "Yes, I agree. It looks perfect. Send a fast rider up ahead to tell cook to stop the chuck wagon close to the center of the valley near the river. Keep the herd movin' down into the valley. Turn the leaders to circle until the herd's forward momentum is stopped and get 'em settled a reasonable distance from where cook stops the chuck wagon. We'll camp tonight near the chuck wagon. Tomorrow we'll see if we need to move. And, tell cook to prepare a special dinner tonight finished off with peach pies."

Ed said, "Yes, sir." He rode off to relay the orders to the crew and send a rider after the cook. He knew they would receive these orders happily. They were exhausted. They needed a short day in the saddle and a good meal, even he and Charles.

The crew brought the herd down into the valley to the river. The cattle spread out along the river's banks, many of them in the shallow water. Most were drinking. The crew rode around the edge of the herd soothing them as they left the water and began eating the long native grass along the banks. The herd didn't need to be circled to stop them. The good grazing did. And, soon, one-by-one, the cattle laid down.

The cook found a good place for the chuck wagon apart from the herd, still near the river, stopped, and set the brake. He and his helper unhitched their team, brushed them, took them to the river to drink, and hobbled them for the evening to graze. They returned to the chuck wagon, climbed up over the front bench into the bed, and threw the crew's bedrolls out onto the ground in a disorganized pile. When the bedrolls were out of the way, they lowered dinner fixings out onto the ground. Finally, they lowered the chuck wagon's tailgate and readied their utensils to prepare the special dinner with peach pie that Charles had requested.

Ed sent several of the hands riding back to the hills to chop down trees to be used for firewood and log benches. When a tree was down, a hand on horseback threw his rope to a hand on the ground who tied the rope to the trunk or the stump of a strong branch. The rider dragged the tree behind his horse to the chuck wagon. Other hands near the chuck wagon chopped or sawed the fallen trees into proper lengths for benches and split the smaller diameter pieces into firewood.

Charles and Ed, along with the few hands not minding the herd, chopping down and dragging trees, or cutting trees into log benches and firewood, sat on the new log benches watching the cook and his helper prepare their dinner. The meal was even better to eat than it smelled while it was being prepared. Charles, Ed, and the whole crew turned in that evening tired and full.

The next morning Charles and Ed ate breakfast separately from the crew. When they finished eating Charles said, "Since I want to grow the herd back to 3,500 head, we'll need a minimum of 50,000 acres, 'bout 15 acres a head, otherwise we'll have to feed 'em over the winter. This valley is about that size. We'll need all of it, includin' the three ranches on the north side. We need their land. We'll have to buy their ranches or force 'em out. Send two scouts to pay 'em a visit. See if they'll leave peaceable."

Ed responded, "I agree, but I think there's more to it. We know there's nothing east of here, we came in that way, but we don't know what's in the other three directions. We don't know if anyone outside the valley owns it or thinks they do. We don't know if you'll have to buy the valley or if you can just claim it. We don't know if there are ranches close by and if they're gonna accept us just movin' in without a fight. I'm sure you'll have to register ownership of this valley with the county. And, we don't know what the closest town is and if we can get the supplies we need there. We need to learn a lot about this country and need to scout out beyond the valley."

Charles considered Ed's comments and replied, "Good thoughts, Ed. We need to learn a lot quickly, but let's take it one step at a time, like peelin' an onion. First, let's find out about the ranches in the valley and if we have any neighbors. As I said before, send two scouts to pay 'em a visit. There and back today. Next, send two scouts west to look for neighborin' ranches. When they're back send two scouts north then south to do the same. Those three trips should take a couple of days each. Go select the scouts for today and get 'em movin'. I want 'em to report directly to me as soon as they get back. I want reports for the next three scouting trips as soon as those scouts get back, too."

Ed had nothing to add, so he said, "Yes sir," and went to find the scouts. He found the scout Harold having coffee at the chuck wagon. He briefed Harold about today's visits to the three ranches at the north side of the valley and the following three scouting trips. He told Harold that he was to take the lead on all four trips and to choose a second scout to go with him, a different one on each trip. He impressed upon Harold the type of information he was to gather, that he was not be seen while scouting the neighboring ranches, and that he was to report to Charles and him as soon as he returned from each trip.

Harold replied, "Yes, we can do the visits and scoutin' trips. We'll talk to each of the ranchers at the north side of the valley today and give them your message and we'll make sure we're not seen on the other three trips. Those three trips'll probably be three days each, one day goin', one day observin', and the third day returnin'. I'll report back to you and Charles as soon as I return from each."

Harold went looking for the other four scouts to assign one each to accompany him on one of the four trips. The first scout he ran into was Bob.

"Bob, we're gonna take a ride this mornin' 'cross the valley. Go get a horse ready. I'll be with you in a bit and explain what we're gonna do."

Bob nodded and left to get his gun belt and Colt, his Winchester, and a canteen. He then went to the remuda to select a horse and get it ready.

Harold found Jon, Lefty, and Snake sitting on logs near the chuck wagon. The logs had been arranged in concentric circles around where the campfire would be built in the evenings.

Harold said, "We're gonna make three trips to scout the neighborin' ranches over the next ten days. We're first goin' west, then north, then south. Each trip'll be three days. You'll each accompany me on one of the trips, first Jon, then Lefty, then Snake. Jon, you and I'll leave first thing in the mornin' the day after tomorrow. Be ready."

Harold left them and went to get his gun belt and Colt, his Winchester, and a canteen. He also went to the remuda to select a horse and get it ready.

Harold and Bob rode out of camp toward the north side of the valley at a walk and soon pushed their horses into a trot. After about an hour they arrived at the first of the three ranches. As they rode up to the corral next to the pole barn, the rancher straightened up from working on a horse's off hind hoof. They didn't see anyone else outside the small cabin or in its window looking out.

The rancher said, "Mornin'. Can I hep ya?"

"Yes," said Harold. "We're scouts for the Bar CS brand that moved into the middle of the valley with 2,000 head of cattle yesterday. Perhaps you noticed us. We're gonna need the whole valley, includin' your ranch. We'll give you a fair price for it. We'd 'preciate it if you'd be ready to leave tomorrow when we come back."

"What if I'm not?"

"We'll help you."

"I'll think about it. Now git."

"We'll be back tomorrow 'bout the same time. Be ready to leave."

The rancher scowled at them, but didn't say anything.

Harold and Bob turned their horses away from the corral and pushed them into a slow trot headed for the second ranch. At the second and third ranches, they had similar exchanges with apparently the solitary male inhabitants.

Harold and Bob returned to their camp late in the afternoon, took their horses to the remuda, and went to find Charles and Ed to report. Harold said to Charles and Ed, "The ranchers are men apparently livin' alone. We only saw a few head of cattle, a wagon, and a team of horses at each of the ranches. Each rancher was defiant about bein' told he'd have to sell or be helped off his land, but we believe they'll sell rather than fight. They each said they'd think about sellin', but we believe they'll go soon as some money is put into their hands."

Charles, Ed, and three scouts, Harold, Bob, Snake, visited the three ranches at the north side of the valley the next day. Their number persuaded the ranchers they were serious. Each of the ranchers understood the threat, and without argument, agreed to sell and leave immediately. Each rancher was allowed to keep his wagon and team, a riding horse, personal items, and supplies. Basically, what they could fit into their wagons. Ed and the three scouts helped the ranchers load their wagons. Charles paid each rancher in cash as he left.

On the way back to camp, Charles said to Ed, "I'm glad we didn't have to use force or kill any of 'em. It was bad enough we forced 'em to sell and leave, but if we'd killed one or more and it was found out, we'd be in trouble with the law, if there is any here 'bouts."

Ed replied, "We don't know where they've gone or if they'll tell anyone what happened. We still could be in trouble if the law finds out what we done."

# 14

Alexander, Lacy, and I were having a quiet breakfast at the Café Madrid. We didn't have much to do in town at the moment. Sunrise had been peaceful for the past month, except for the usual nighttime drunken spats at the saloons. Even the whores were keeping a low profile, just doing their business without bothering anyone. Life was beginning to feel downright civilized, normal, and routine.

Ward walked through the front door, apparently looking for us, because as soon as he saw us, he came directly to our table. He said, "Can I join you? I just heard somethin' you should know."

Alexander replied, "Of course, Ward, please do. Coffee?"

Ward said, "Yes, please," as he sat.

Alexander motioned to the Spaniard to bring Ward coffee and we all waited for Ward to continue.

After Ward had his coffee and took a couple of sips, he said, "I was in the Chicago House drinkin' with a couple of locals and a drifter. The drifter told us 'bout a large cattle drive he'd seen a week or so ago coming this way from the east. From his description, it was movin' west toward the Runnin' Bird."

I said, "Do you know anythin' more specific, like how big a herd, how many crew, and who's the trail boss?"

Ward answered, "The drifter said it was a large herd and it looked like there were somewhere near 20 in the crew."

"Is the drifter still at the Chicago House?" Alexander asked.

Ward said, "No. He said he was on his way to Trinidad and was in a hurry to get there. I came directly here lookin' for you. We all know you have breakfast here every mornin'."

Alexander looked at me and Lacy and said, "Maybe we should breeze the horses this morning over to the Runnin' Bird and see what's up with Bird and Claire. Could be we learn some more 'bout this."

"When you get back, stop at the Chicago House and tell me what you learned," Ward said rising from his chair. He nodded to us and left.

We finished breakfast and Alexander paid. We left the Café Madrid and walked to the marshal's office in City Hall to get our Winchesters, my eight-gauge, ammunition, canteens, jackets, and slickers. We passed by Alexander's house and packed our own lunch. We didn't want to take a chance on what we'd get if we'd let Ella do it. Finally, we walked to the livery, readied our horses, and took the north road out of Sunrise.

It was a beautiful late summer day, not too hot or humid. We and the horses were anxious to move out. We walked the horses a while to warm them up, trotted a ways, and cantered some. We alternated walking, trotting, and cantering to keep the horses rested and eat up the miles. We soon approached the meadow just above the Running Bird where we usually found the appaloosa stallion and his mares. We were disappointed this morning, they weren't there. So, instead of riding around the meadow on the crest of the hill as we normally did, we rode through the middle of the meadow and dropped down the hill on the other side to the ranch.

We rode directly to the main house, dismounted, watered the horses, and tied them to the hitching rail. Bird and John must have seen us coming down the hill, because they came over from the barn to meet us.

Alexander started the greetings, "Mornin', Bird, John."

"Mornin', marshal, deputies," replied Bird.

Lacy and I nodded our greeting.

John said, "Mornin'. I'd like to stay and talk, but we been carin' for a mare and its newborn foal. I have to get back to 'em." John nodded good bye, turned toward the barn, and walked briskly away without waiting for a response.

Bird invited us onto the porch for coffee. After we were seated, he went into the house, told Claire we were there, and came back outside to sit with us while we waited for Claire and the coffee. We passed the time talking about the ranch. We heard news about the herd, remuda, range, and how he and Claire were being accepted by their hands and the neighboring ranchers. Everything we heard was positive. We were happy for them and proud of the way they were progressing.

We all stood when Claire came out of the house onto the porch followed by José. Claire carried a tray with four mugs, and rolls. José carried a large pot of coffee. They set the tray and coffee on the table.

Claire ran to Alexander and gave him a big hug and whispered in his ear. He whispered back and they both smiled. She turned to me and Lacy and smiled again. We sat as José poured coffee for us then went back into the house.

Alexander looked at me indicating I should start the conversation. I said to Bird, "Have you heard anythin' 'bout a large herd of cattle comin' this way?"

Bird answered, "Yes, one of the ranchers from the valley to the east came by a couple days ago on his way to Trinidad. He was very upset. Seems a large herd was driven into his valley. He was visited by two of the crew askin' questions the next day. And, a day later, five men came. They said they needed his ranch and offered to buy it. He didn't think he had a choice, but to sell. He figured sellin' was healthier than saying no. Four of 'em helped him pack his wagon, the fifth one paid him. He figured the one who paid him was the boss. He said the other two ranchers in the valley was moved out before him, though they left in the other direction, toward the east."

Alexander asked, "Have they been here? Have you seen 'em?"

Bird said, "They haven't been here, but we've seen a couple of hands sittin' their horses on top of the hill to the east. I've been meanin' to ride up there and take a look down into the valley."

Alexander said, "Whyn't we do that now. But, we're just lookin'. We've no jurisdiction here and we've no proof they've done anythin' wrong."

We walked to our horses and waited for Bird to ready his. When he brought his horse out of the barn, we mounted, rode together to the top of the hill east of the ranch, and looked into the valley to the east. It was a large nearly round valley with good grass, large trees scattered throughout, ringed with forested low hills, and a shallow river running through its middle. In the middle of the valley along the river was the herd which looked to number around 2,000 head. There were some hands with the herd watching them and keeping them quiet.

Lacy said, "Quiet down there. They're mindin' their own business. We've got no call to bother 'em. And we shouldn't meet 'em up close until we have to."

I replied, "I agree. I think we should leave before they get a good look at us. It may make our lives more difficult if they're able to recognize us before we want 'em to."

Alexander nodded in agreement. We turned our horses, rode back down the hill, and returned to the Running Bird. We said goodbye to Bird and Claire and left for Sunrise.

We got back to Sunrise at sunset, settled the horses at the livery, and went directly to the marshal's office in City Hall. Finding everything in order, we walked the length of Main Street, visiting the saloons along the way. We came last to the Chicago House, where we had dinner with Ward.

When we had finished eating, I said to Ward, "We rode out to visit Bird and Claire today. They're doin' well. They've seen riders on the crest of the hill to their east, but haven't been bothered by 'em. We rode up to the crest of the hill and looked into the valley. We saw a large herd and some riders. Either they didn't notice us or didn't care we were up there watchin' 'em."

Alexander said, "So far, don't seem they've done anythin' illegal. And, since it's outside of Sunrise, it's not our jurisdiction. Guess we'll leave 'em alone, for now."

Ward said, "Thanks for followin' up and looking into this. I 'preciate it." He signaled for Clay to bring us a bottle of whisky and glasses. We each had a glass of whiskey to end the day.

# 15

The scouts returned from trips to ranches north, south, and west of their valley in the late afternoons, three days apart, over the next nine days. When they returned from each trip, they cared for their horses then reported to Charles and Ed what they'd seen: a total of ten working ranches with large herds, large crews, substantial houses, bunk houses, corrals, and barns. The ranches appeared peaceful, guards weren't posted, and the hands they saw weren't carrying firearms, Colts or Winchesters.

The morning of the tenth day, while Charles and Ed were having breakfast, Charles said, "I've been thinkin' 'bout what the scouts told us. Seems to me the neighborin' ranches would be easy pickin's for rustlers. We could form teams of three, a scout and two hands. We've got five scouts, that's five teams, 15 hands. There are 22 of us, 18 when you remove the cook and his helper and you and me. We've got enough hands. Each team goes once a week, that's teams out five nights a week. They'll be looking for and bringin' back stray bunches of cattle from the neighborin' ranches."

Ed nodded he understood.

Charles continued, "Considerin' the distances to the neighboring ranches, teams would leave in the afternoons to arrive after sundown. They'd have to find a bunch of cattle and head directly back, drivin' the bunch in the dark to reach here before sunrise."

Ed said, "I think it can be done."

"We vary the direction so we don't establish a pattern. A ranch should not be visited too often. And, no more than 20 head should be brought back from a ranch on a single trip. The ranches probably won't notice 20 or fewer head missin' at a time. In a couple of months we could collect 500 or more head."

Ed replied, "I like it. It's an easy and fast way to grow the herd, but it's rustlin'. I'm sure the scouts won't have a problem with it, but I'm not sure 'bout the hands. And, it could be a problem for us down the line."

"I've thought 'bout that. First, most of our hands'll probably rustle if we pay 'em extra for it, but all hands'd have to be in on it. Those that'd refuse would have to be removed from the ranch before we could start. Second, future problems won't come up if we're smart and cover our tracks correctly."

"OK, but how do we identify those who'll refuse without tippin' our hand and what should we do about 'em?"

"You should know the hands well enough by now to identify those who'll refuse. Figure it out today, pay 'em off and get 'em out of here by tomorrow morning. We can't have 'em around to overhear anything 'bout this."

"Yes, sir."

Charles hesitated a while thinking, then continued, "I'll pay a dollar bonus for each head brought in. I'll put the bonus money in a pot the same evening the cattle are brought in and tallied. The bonus money will be shared equally by all hands and distributed at the end of each week. You get rid of those who won't rustle tomorrow mornin' and we'll send the first team out tomorrow afternoon. You've got some preparation to do. You'd better get to it."

"Yes, I'd better.  I think the first ones to go will be the ones who wanted to return to Murphyville once we settled somewhere. The next ones to go will be those who aren't aggressive enough to rustle.  I'll talk with the scouts and the most trustworthy hands and make team assignments.  I'll send the first team tomorrow afternoon to the ranch to the west, the next afternoon the second team to a ranch to the north, and the next afternoon, the third team to a ranch to the south.  I don't think a team will bring in many head on its first trip.  They'll be learnin' where the cattle are and safe trails around the ranches."

Charles replied, "You're right.  Good thoughts.  Get it goin'."

Ed went to the chuck wagon, got a fresh cup of coffee and thought about how to cull the hands who wouldn't take part in rustling.  He was pondering this when he decided he may not have to release anyone.  He had another idea.

Ed went looking for Charles and found him at the remuda checking the horses with the wrangler.  Ed said, "Charles, can we talk?"

"Sure Ed, give me a minute, I'll be right with you."

Ed waited until Charles was free and they could talk privately.  He motioned for Charles to walk with him and said to him when they were a ways from the wrangler, "Charles, here's some ideas.  If you remember, two of our hands didn't want to stay with us once we found the place to settle, they wanted to return to Murphyville.  Since we seem to have found our place and are settlin', they can be let go.  I'll send 'em out of here tomorrow mornin'."

Charles nodded.

"There are three hands I'm sure won't go along with our new plans, but they're good workers. We could send them to the ranches on the north side of the valley. They could farm, raise vegetables for us, you know we gotta eat something other than beef all the time. They could also take care of the wagons, mend tack, build things. It would isolate 'em from the rustlin', but keep 'em with us. They're good, solid hands. I'll send 'em out of here tomorrow mornin', too."

"Ed, great ideas. Get started."

"Charles, I'll be sending five hands out of here, leaving 13 for the rustlin' teams. That's three teams of three and one team of four. One team will have to go out twice every week."

"I'm sure it won't be a problem, Ed."

Ed left Charles to find the two hands who said they wanted to return to Murphyville. When he found them he said, "We've arrived where we're gonna stay. You two wanted to return to Murphyville when we finished the drive and we're done. Hope you haven't changed your minds, 'cause we don't need you anymore. Pack your gear and be ready to leave tomorrow mornin' right after breakfast. You can take your saddle horses, tack, bedrolls, and personals. See the cook for some supplies and a few cooking utensils, if you'll need 'em. And, you can have a pack horse. Come see me in the mornin' when you're ready to leave and I'll pay you what you're owed."

"Thank you, we're happy to leave, to go home" said one of them.

"We'll be ready to go first thing in the mornin'," said the other.

They wandered away whooping excitedly about going back to Texas. Ed smiled, thinking how happy he'd made them, and began looking for the three hands to send to the small ranches at the north side of the valley.

Ed found them sitting on the logs encircling the dying embers of the morning campfire, drinking coffee. Ed sat with them and said, "We've ended our drive and we're gonna settle here. We don't need as many hands to handle the herd. We're gonna let you three go. If you wanna stay with us, we've got new jobs for you, farmin', maintainin' equipment, and buildin' things. Your new jobs will be at the ranches at the north side of the valley. Do you want to stay with us?"

"Yes," they replied in unison.

"Good. Your new jobs start immediately. You're to leave tomorrow mornin' after breakfast. You'll take one of the escort wagons with an extra team, your saddle horses and an extra saddle horse each, tack, bedrolls, and personals. See the cook to collect supplies, cooking utensils, and seeds for the crops he'll want you to grow. Also, collect tools and leather repair and carpentry supplies. Get started."

The three hands first went to pack their personals. Their second stop was to see the cook for supplies, cooking utensils, and seeds. Their third stop was for tools and leather repair and carpentry supplies. Their fourth stop was to select an escort wagon, load their personals, tools, and supplies into it, and ready it for their departure the following morning. When they finished loading the wagon, they had two chores left, they needed to collect the harness for the wagon team and isolate the team and an extra team so in the morning they could hitch up and leave without delay. They finished just before dinner. During their preparations, they became more excited about their new jobs.

After breakfast the next morning, two hands left on their mounts leading a pack horse headed for Texas and another three hitched a team to the front of the loaded escort wagon, tied an extra team to its rear, and left for the ranches at the north side of the valley. One hand drove the wagon, the other two rode behind the extra team leading four riding horses, one for the hand driving the wagon and three extras.

Ed watched the two groups of men leave. He'd already considered rustling team assignments for the remaining hands and changes to the daily work schedules the rustling would cause. To create the first three teams, he assigned one scout and two hands. The fourth team had two scouts and two hand. He decided to introduce the rustling, team assignments, and new schedules at lunch.

When all hands had assembled at the chuck wagon for lunch, Ed stood and said, "Give me your attention."

When everyone was quiet, Ed continued, "Charles has decided to settle here, in this valley. His priotity is growin' the herd back to the size it was before we left Murphyville, and in time, expandin' the ranch beyond the confines of the valley. To grow the herd, we can do it the normal way, droppin' calves or buyin' cattle. Or, we can do it faster by takin' cattle from our neighbors. Charles likes the last method, it's quicker and cheaper. We'll be gatherin' strays from the surroundin' ranches at night, startin' tonight, five nights a week. All of you'll be ridin' out in teams of three or four to collect strays from the neighborin' ranches. Charles will pay a dollar bonus for each head you bring back. The bonus money will be shared by all hands in camp, includin' the cook and his helper. Anyone object to this or won't participate?"

Ed waited, no-one responded, so he continued, "To be frank, this is rustlin'. If you're caught you're goin' to be in serious trouble and so is our outfit, so be careful. They hang rustlers. If you come across anyone, leave any cattle you've got and disappear into the night. Don't shoot anyone unless you've no other choice. If you shoot someone, you and your team don't come back here. Ever. Questions?"

Again, no-one responded, so Ed continued, "The team assignments are posted on the side of the chuck wagon. New work schedules for everyone are also posted there. I'll announce the team for the day and the direction it'll go at lunch. Questions?"

Again, no-one responded, so Ed continued, "Today's team will be lead by Snake. Bill and Pike, you'll go with him. Your target is the ranch west of us. You're to leave in 'bout two hours, to be there after sundown. Remember, look for strays, cattle away from the main herd, and don't come back with more'n 20 head. If you have any questions you don't want to ask now or come up with later, come see me."

After breakfast the next morning, Snake got a fresh cup of coffee and sat next to Ed. He said, "Last night when we found the main herd it was pretty dark. It looked huge, as many cattle as there were stars in the sky. We chose a small bunch off to the side, maybe 16 or 17 head. We collected 'em and started drivin' 'em back here when a yearling come running up from out a nowhere bawling 'take me, take me.' So, we did."

# 16

When Alexander and I first started several years ago in Sunrise as marshal and deputy, we would sit watching Main Street from the covered boardwalk in front of the old marshal's office. When we were security for the saloons, we would sit watching Main Street from the covered boardwalk in front of the Chicago House. Now that we and Lacy are marshal and deputies, we sit watching Main Street from the covered boardwalk in front of City Hall, where the new marshal's office is. We do the same jobs, but where we sit watching Main Street has changed. Not sure which location has the better view, but seems to me, the same number of pretty women come by here as did at the previous two.

We'd been sitting on the covered boardwalk in front of City Hall watching Main Street and talking for some 20 minutes since breakfast at the Café Madrid when I noticed Bird standing next to me. His horse was tied at the hitching rail, but neither he or his horse had made a sound, they'd just appeared. I weren't startled to see him. He appears out a nowhere frequently.

I said, "Mornin' Bird."

Alexander turned his head and nodded at Bird.

Bird nodded at us.

Surprised, Lacy jerked sideways to face Bird and said, "I'll never get used to you. You're a ghost."

Bird said, "White man sleeps with eyes open. Miss everything."

I said, "Drag up a chair and sit a spell."

Bird went into the marshal's office, brought a chair back outside with him, and sat leaning against the wall, as we were.

I waited the appropriate amount of time then asked, "Bird, why're you here?"

Bird waited the appropriate amount of time and replied, "Since you come to the Runnin' Bird, maybe five weeks ago, I've seen men among the trees at the top of the hill east of the ranch. They appear, sit their horses and watch us a while, then leave. They've come several times, but haven't come down to the ranch. Don't know why they come or what they want. It bothers me. Claire's very disturbed."

He was quiet a while, then continued, "Since the last time I seen 'em, we've noticed cattle missing on six occasions. Six small bunches, maybe 90 head total. I found hoof prints from three shod horses where each bunch should've been. Horse hoof prints go east with the cattle toward the valley where the new outfit is. I need your help."

"Bird, officially, we've no jurisdiction outside of Sunrise. You're in County Deputy Sheriff Knight's jurisdiction. But, that don't mean we can't help you, it just makes it more complicated. Has the same been happening to any of the other ranchers near you?"

"Don't know."

"Bird, you need to do a couple of things right away. First, send riders to the ranches north and south of you and find out if this is happening to them, too. Second, find out if your missing cattle are in the new herd east of you."

Bird thought for a minute, then answered, "I'll send riders tomorrow north and south, not east. My hands aren't Chiricahua. They make too much noise to send east into that herd. Chiricahua are quiet. We're able to see brands in the dark. I can't do it alone, it'd be too risky alone. I'll have to go home to the res and bring back more Chiricahua."

Alexander said, "Bird, if you bring Chiricahua here, will they do only what you tell 'em?"

"Yes."

"How many will come?"

"Bring five for sure."

"Good, five's enough. We'll find Knight and get him here and meet you at the Runnin' Bird in three weeks. Since today's Sunday, means we'll be at the Running Bird the third Sunday from today."

Bird nodded.

Alexander turned to Lacy and said, "Lacy, take tomorrow's mornin' train to Trinidad and see Knight. Tell him what appears to be happenin' and we need his help. Be sure he understands it's in his jurisdiction and we'll back him completely if he deputizes us. Be back as soon as you can."

Lacy replied, "OK, I'll be on tomorrow mornin's train."

We relaxed now that a plan was in place, sat quietly, drinking coffee, and watching Main Street. Not much going on this morning, a slow day. Several men on horses went by, two alone and a few in small groups, and a couple of wagons loaded with freshly cut lumber from the saw mill rumbled past.

We were close to dozing until we saw two women on the other side of the street walking in front of the Chicago House, fancy dresses, painted up. We recognized them immediately, Sabrina White and Stella Penn.

I said to Alexander, "What's Ella doing dressed like that out here on Main Street with Sabrina this time a day?"

Alexander focused on Ella and jumped up out of his chair. He stepped off the boardwalk and walked slowly and deliberately across the street toward her. I followed. Lacy and Bird remained in their chairs.

Sabrina saw Alexander crossing the street toward them. She took Ellas' arm and they stopped. Both she and Ella were looking toward Alexander and me, but seeing only Alexander, as he and I stepped up on the boardwalk in front of them.

Alexander tipped his hat and said, "Mornin' ladies."

They gave Alexander slight curtseys, and Sabrina replied, "Good mornin', Mr. Gadson."

I said, "Mornin' ladies. It's a beautiful mornin' for a stroll. Are you ladies goin' anywhere in particular?"

Sabrina replied, "Good mornin', Mr. Masters, why yes we are. We're going to the Café Madrid for coffee and biscuits and then to my house. I'm going to show Mrs. Penn all the changes I've made to make my house more comfortable now that I'm alone."

I responded, "I can understand how lonely it must be for you in that big house, Mrs. White, now that Aldus is gone."

"Oh, it is Mr. Masters," replied Sabrina, "dreadfully lonely. You know, you and Mr. Gadson are welcome to visit me anytime."

Alexander said, "Mrs. White, thank you for your kind invitation. And Mrs. Penn, is she welcome, too?"

"Of course she is," replied Sabrina enthusiastically. "I hope Mrs. Penn comes to my house often. She can stay with me at my house as long as it pleases her."

"Of course I will, Sabrina," said Ella. "I intend to spend a lot of time with you at your house."

Turning to Alexander, Ella added, "Mrs. White is my closest and dearest friend. She and I have so much in common. Bein' with her makes me feel much better about myself and who I am. With Claire gone and you off marshallin' so much, I'm mostly alone. You and I are only together at your house and when we're together there I'm still alone. I'm witherin' like a dying flower. I need to blossom again. I need excitement in my life. I need to fill my days, and nights, with people. People who appreciate me. I intend to spend a lot of time with Sabrina at her house, with her friends."

I could see that Alexander was really surprised by what he was hearing. Though he looked as stoic as ever, I could tell he was very upset by the set of his jaw and the intensity of his stare. I knew there was no way Alexander could respond to what Ella had said. I've never known him able to express his feelings to anyone, especially to a woman in front of an audience.

Since not one of us seemed to want to say anything more, I jumped in, "Ladies, we hope you have a pleasant day. Alexander and I have business to attend to here in town. Good-bye."

I took Alexander's arm, turned him, and guided him back across the street. Once there, we joined Lacy and Bird on the boardwalk sitting against the wall. Not one of us spoke.

Finally I said, "Appears the coyote can't change its howl."

Alexander replied, "Seems so. Guess we'll just have to wait and see what develops."

At that, Bird stood up, nodded at Alexander then at Lacy and me, stepped off the boardwalk to the hitching rail, untied his horse, mounted, and rode out of town at a slow trot.

# 17

The northbound train was scheduled to arrive in Sunrise at 11:00AM, but in practice it arrived anytime between 10:00AM and noon. To be certain not to miss it, Lacy was at the station at 9:30AM. He'd rather wait two and one-half hours for the train than miss it, especially today.

Lacy was wise to have been early because the train was earlier than ever It arrived just a few minutes after he did. He boarded and settled in to sleep for as much of the three hour trip as he could and was asleep when the train arrived in Trinidad. The conductor awakened him as the train stopped.

Lacy said, "Thank you for awakening me. Do you know where the sheriff's office is?"

"Yes," the conductor replied. "Go down Chestnut Street to Main Street and turn right. It'll be a couple of doors down on the right side of the street. You can't miss it."

Lacy nodded to the conductor, climbed down to the station platform, and followed the conductor's directions to the sheriff's office. The office was occupied by a single person wearing a badge and a gun belt and sitting at a large round table in the center of the room. There were four chairs at the table, the one the person was sitting in and three others. No two of the chairs were alike and all four were listing in one direction or another. The only other furniture in the room was a rifle cabinet with five new looking, shinny Winchesters and a shotgun in it.

Lacy said, "Afternoon. I'm Deputy Lacy Burnham from Sunrise. I'm here to see Deputy Knight."

The deputy replied, "Afternoon. I'm Deputy George Every. Deputy Knight is out with the sheriff. They're checking on some trouble at a ranch north a town. I expect Deputy Knight to be back first thing in the mornin' day after tomorrow. You could leave a message for him with me, or if you have to speak to him, you'll have to come back then."

"Yes, I have to speak directly to him," said Lacy. "I guess I'll have to wait around here in Trinidad for him to return. Where can I get good meals and a room for a couple of nights?"

The Deputy replied, "I can recommend both. We're on Main Street. Turn right goin' out of the office. The first street you come to is Maple, the second Commerce. At the northeast corner of Main and Commerce is Sweet's Café. They have the best food in town. Make sure your badge is showin', you may get your meals free. There's a hotel next to Sweet's."

Lacy took Every's advice about Sweet's Café and the hotel. He had good meals and two good nights sleep. He returned to the sheriff's office midmorning two days later. Deputy Knight was waiting for him.

Knight said, "Mornin', Lacy. Heard you'd been here lookin' for me. I'm sorry you had to wait. You're lookin' fit and prosperous. Why're you so far from home?"

Lacy replied, "I feel fit, though I can't say much about prosperous."

He hesitated briefly, then continued, "Alexander sent me to see you. We're havin' trouble northeast of Sunrise. An outfit's moved into a valley east of the Runnin' Bird with a large herd and they appear to be rustlin' from 'em and other ranches in the area. It's outside our jurisdiction, but within your's. We could handle it ourselves, but may not be legal. We want you there with us and we want you to deputize us. We'd appreciate it if you'd come to Sunrise in 16 days, two weeks from this Friday. Saturday, we'll plan what we're goin' to do. And Sunday, we're to be at the Runnin' Bird. On the way back I'm stoppin' in Penance to talk with Dyson and Jackson to ask them to join us in Sunrise, too."

Knight answered, "You bet, I'll be there. I'll bring another deputy with me, one who needs experience with problems like this. You met him when you first come in, Deputy Every. Is that OK?"

"Yes," responded Lacy. "We could use another lawman. As far as I know, there'll be Alexander, Emmett, and me, Dyson and Jackson, you and Every, and Bird and five Chiricahua he's supposed to be bringin' from the reservation. We should be 13 against 'bout 20. Actually eight against 'bout 20, 'cause I don't think the Chiricahua will fight. They'll be more of 'em than us, but we'll sure have 'em out gunned."

Knight replied, "OK. We'll be there on the afternoon train 16 days from today, two weeks from this coming Friday. Now, I've got business to attend, I have to be going."

Lacy stood, shook Knight's extended hand, and left the sheriff's office for the train station. There was plenty of time before the afternoon train south to Penance, but the schedule couldn't be trusted. He went to the station early.

When he climbed down from the train onto the platform in Penance, it was the middle of the afternoon and Penance was busy. The last time he had been there it had been a sleepy little town. Today, there were a lot of people going every direction on foot, on horses, and in wagons. Every store and saloon had its share of customers.

Lacy found the marshal's office and went in. Dyson and Jackson were sitting across from each other at a round table in the middle of the room. There were two empty chairs at the table and a bottle of whisky and several glasses in the center of the table between them.

Gregory Jackson motioned to one of the empty chairs and said, "I was hopin' someone would come in just 'bout now. I need a person that talks back. Talkin' with Dyson is like talkin' with a cigar store Indian."

Jackson poured some whisky into a glass for Lacy and continued, "What brings you north to Penance?"

Lacy sipped the whisky and replied, "Actually, I'm on my way back south to Sunrise. I've been to Trinidad to see Knight 'bout a problem and I'm here to see you 'bout it, too."

Lacy took another sip of whisky and continued, "We're having trouble northeast of Sunrise with an outfit that's moved into the valley east of the Runnin' Bird and appears to be rustlin' from 'em and other ranches in the area. Knight's agreed to come down with another deputy to help us, it's his jurisdiction, and we'd like you there with us. If you were with us, we'll still be out numbered, but not out gunned."

Jackson replied, "We're with you, gladly. Things've been too durn quiet here lately. It's getting' real boring. We need some excitement. We'll be ready to leave tomorrow mornin'."

Lacy answered, "Thank you, but not so fast. We need you in Sunrise 16 days from today. That's two weeks from this comin'

Friday. Saturday, we'll plan what we're goin' to do. And Sunday, we're to be at the Runnin' Bird to get ready to do it."

Jackson replied, "OK. We'll be there. Now it's time to make our afternoon rounds, have dinner, and get some sleep. Come along with us. You can come back here after dinner and sleep in one of the cells. I'm sure you've nothin' else to do until the southbound train to Sunrise tomorrow afternoon."

# 18

Charles and Ed rode from the Bar CS valley to Sunrise the same morning Lacy took the train from Sunrise to Trinidad. Charles and Ed went to Sunrise to gather information about the town and the availability of the supplies they'd need to build their new ranch. They also had three personal reasons for their trip. It had been months since they'd been in a saloon. It had been months since they'd eaten food prepared by anyone other than their cook. And, it had been months since they'd been with women. They were interested in gathering the information they needed for the ranch, but were excited by the prospects of satisfying their personal desires.

They left their camp in the middle of the valley east of the Running Bird just after sunrise, rode to the crest of the hills to the south, rode west along the crest, and dropped down onto the road west of the Running Bird. They arrived in Sunrise just after noon.

They rode directly to the livery and put up their horses. When they left the livery, they carried only their saddle bags with changes of clothes and their personals, since they intended to spend a night or two in a hotel with real beds and wouldn't need anything else.

Walking along Main Street, they looked in but didn't linger in two small saloons. They looked in the Silver Chalet, found it better, but thought it lacked the atmosphere they were looking for. When they looked in the Chicago House, they were delighted, it met their expectations. This was a real saloon. They felt at home as soon as they were inside.

They went to the bar, got a bottle of whisky and two glasses from Clay, went to an empty table, and sat. Ed poured each of them a generous glassful of whisky and they settled very happily into their chairs. They drank their first glassful quickly and Ed poured them each another. Their second glassful, they could savor. They began noticing people around them who were drinking, eating, playing cards, sitting and flirting with whores, talking, and laughing. This was what had been missing the last several months.

Charles returned to the bar and asked Clay, "Can you serve us dinner at our table?"

Clay replied, "Of course. We have a fixed menu. You get whatever we have, probably steak, potatoes, bread, butter, and gravy. One dollar each."

Charles answered, "Wonderful. The faster you can get it to us the better. We've been looking forward to a meal like this for months."

Alexander and I walked into the Chicago House and found an empty table as Charles was walking back to his table. As we sat we spread our coats away from the handles of our Colts. I stood my eight-gauge against the chair next to me.

Alexander said, "Notice the stranger?"

I nodded.

"Recognize him?"

"Familiar, but can't place him."

"Me, too."

Clay brought us a bottle of whisky and glasses and said, "Evening, Alexander, Emmett. If you want to see Ward, he should be here later, but I don't know exactly when."

Alexander said, "Thank you, Clay, but we're not here to see Ward. We just need a drink, or two, to end the day."

I scanned the room looking for anything unusual. Nothing was amiss, but I stared intently at the two new faces at a table across the room. I studied them for a short time and looked at Alexander. He nodded, signaling he had studies them, too, but he didn't say anything.

Ed leaned close to Charles and said quietly, "Did you notice who just came in and sat, the marshal and his deputy. Do you recognize 'em?"

"You betcha," Charles responded. "The marshal is Alexander Gadson and the deputy is Emmett Masters. They worked together in Marfa a couple of years ago. We knew 'bout 'em there and I surely do remember 'em. Alexander's one of the best, if not the best, gun hand ever. Emmett's probably as good with a handgun, but he carries that eight-gauge. He's lethal with it."

"In our valley, we're outside their jurisdiction, aren't we? Do you think they'll help the ranchers near our valley anyway?"

"Don't know. They may if the ranchers are their friends. Though I'm sure they could contact the county sheriff and work under his jurisdiction."

Clay brought their dinners and Charles and Ed began eating, which interrupted their conversation until they'd finished.

Ed said, "If you remember the reasons for this trip, we've completed all but one of 'em. We need to meet some women. Any ideas?"

Charles answered, "Yes, go ask the bartender if there's a gentlemen's club with clean, pretty women and a good, quiet atmosphere."

Ed replied, "Good idea," and went to the end of the bar, away from other customers, so as not to be heard and signaled Clay to come talk with him.

Clay walked down the bar to where Ed was standing and said, "Can I help you?"

Ed said, "Yes, you can. Is there a good, quiet gentlemen's club in town with clean, pretty women?"

"We've got clean, pretty women here. Take your pick from them at the table in the back. And, we've got nice, quiet rooms upstairs."

"We was thinking 'bout somewhere more discrete."

"Well, yes, there is one. It just opened. It's called Bellas. I haven't been there, but I know the two women who opened it, they're pretty, and they keep themselves very presentable. Their names are Sabrina White and Ella Penn. They use Sabrina's house. Don't know anything else. Please don't tell anyone I told you 'bout Bellas."

Ed got directions and returned to sit with Charles. He said, "Seems there is a gentlemen's club should suit us a short walk from here. The bartender knows the two women who run the place, gave me directions, but doesn't know much about it except the women are clean, pretty, and presentable. You ready?"

"Absolutely," said Charles. "We've finished dinner and our glasses are empty. Nothin' holding us here. I'll settle up and we'll go."

They left the Chicago House following the directions Ed received from Clay and soon arrived at what should have been Bellas. They climbed onto the porch and Ed knocked on the door.

After a brief time, the door opened. Standing in the open doorway was a short, thick man holding a ten-gauge shotgun. He said, "State your names and business here."

Ed replied, "I'm Ed Vargas and this here is Charles Stockett. We're here to be in the company of women. Are we at the right place?"

"Yes you are, provided you mind your manners. First, I'll take your guns and knives. You'll get them back when you leave. Then you can go into the parlor and get comfortable."

Charles said, "We're not heeled. We had to turn in our weapons at the saloon."

The man in the doorway answered, "Good. Town rules. People don't carry no weapons in town, we don't have no shootings or stabbings in town. Come on in. My name's Gerald Kroutsch. I'm the bouncer, security, bartender, cook, swamper, and maid. You need anythin', see me."

Ed and Charles went into the parlor and sat on an overstuffed, dark purple, velvet couch. After they were seated, a pretty, young women came into the room carrying a tray with a bottle of whiskey and three glasses. She poured some whiskey in each of the glasses, gave Ed and Charles each a glass, and picked up the third.

She said, "My name is Kati Madri. I'm here to make sure you gentlemen get started on a very pleasant and memorable evening. Sabrina and Ella will join us shortly. So, for the moment, there's just you and me. How can I entertain you?"

# 19

Charles and Ed returned to their valley refreshed and happy. They had learned what they needed to know about the town of Sunrise and had satisfied their three personal reasons for going there.

They had been gone two nights. During their absence, Harold, their lead scout had been in charge. He and the rest of their hands had kept the herd quiet and brought in another 32 head from neighboring ranches.

The following morning Ed had breakfast with Harold. Ed said, "You're the person I've been able to count on most since you joined us. You're dependable and conscientious. You're goin' to be the first to go into town for a couple of days away from us and the herd. You can select two hands to go with you. I recommend two saloons to visit, the Silver Chalet and the Chicago House. There's another diversion you might also enjoy, Bellas. They have a couple of pretty, clean women. You can leave this mornin' and be back two days from today in the afternoon."

Harold replied, "Thank you. I sure could use some time away from the herd, a real saloon, some excitement. I'm sure the hands I take with me will feel the same."

"Take care in town. The marshal and his deputy are two of the best gun hands anywhere. Charles and I know them from Marfa. Town rules require you not be heeled. You have to turn in your guns, Colts and Winchesters, to the marshal or a saloon when you arrive. You can pick 'em up when you leave. Follow the rules. We don't want any trouble. We have to keep a low profile. Understand?"

"I understand. I'll try to control myself and the other two. No guarantee."

"You want to go, there better be a guarantee."

"OK, I hear you. I'll pick two hands and be back two days from now in the afternoon. I'm gone."

Harold walked off considering who to ask to accompany him. He decided he would ask two of the other scouts. There were four to choose from, Bob, Jon, Lefty, and Snake. He would ask the first two he found.

The first two he found were Bob and Lefty near the chuck wagon, sitting on the logs near the dying campfire, drinking coffee, and talking. He said to them, "We three been given the opportunity for a couple of days in town, starting immediately. If you're goin' with me, go get your stuff and saddle up. Now!"

They hurried to get ready, rode out of camp within the hour, and arrived in Sunrise by mid afternoon. They went directly to the livery and put up, watered, and fed their horses. Their next stop was the Silver Chalet.

Harold ordered a bottle of whiskey and three glasses. Their first drink went down quickly. So did their second and third. The three drinks seemed to fill a void, because after the third, they slowed down, sipped their fourth and talked quietly.

During a lull in the conversation, Bob said enthusiastically, "Remember that time in Murphyville when we shot the candle glasses from the chandelier?" Waiting a beat for an answer, but not getting one, he continued, "What do you say we do the same, here, now?"

Harold replied at a whisper, "Bob, Ed made me guarantee we wouldn't get into any trouble. We would keep a low profile. You know what we're doing out there. We can't have the law comin' around our valley."

"Well, Harold," Bob smirked, "we need some excitement. From the looks of this town and the people we've seen so far, we can do whatever we want."

Bob drew his Colt and began shooting at the chandelier. He stopped when his Colt was empty, reloaded, and shot another full load at the chandelier. All the time he was shooting, Harold was screaming at him to stop.

What they didn't notice was that while Bob was shooting at the chandelier, a well dressed man quietly left the saloon. It was Lowell Williams, the saloon' owner. Lowell walked as quickly as he could to the marshal's office in City Hall.

As soon as he entered the marshal's office, Lowell said, "Three men came into the Silver Chalet and are shootin' up the place. Come quickly."

Alexander and I checked our Colts, I grabbed my eight-gauge, and we left City Hall for the Silver Chalet. When we got there, we went quietly through the batwing doors, Alexander to the left and me to the right. We watched the three men at the bar, one with a Colt in his hand, and waited for them to notice they were being watched.

When we were noticed, Alexander said, "Town rules require you turn in your Colts. You didn't. You're creatin' a disturbance here and you causin' a lot of damage. Put your Colt carefully away in its holster. All three of you take your gun belts off, very slowly. Put 'em on the floor directly in front of you and take a step back away from 'em.  Now!  Don't make any quick moves or point a Colt at us.  You won't live long enough to shoot."

The man with his Colt in his hand said, "Marshal, you and your deputy should go back to your office.  We're havin' some fun and we're not goin' to stop."

Alexander replied, "You'll be the first to die.  Emmett over there will kill the other two with his eight-gauge."

We waited.  No-one moved.  The man with the Colt in his hand began lifting it to shoot, but didn't get it far up before Alexander drew his Colt and put a bullet into the center of his chest.  He flew backwards, landing spread eagled on his back and didn't move.  My eight-gauge was already pointed at the other two.  Their Colts were still in their holsters.  They saw they didn't stand a chance and unbuckeled their gun belts, dropped them, and took a step backwards.

Alexander said, "Who are you and where do you come from?"

Harold answered, "I'm Harold, that's Lefty, and Bob's on the floor.  We work a herd for Charles Stockett in the valley east of the Runnin' Bird."

Alexander replied, "Bob caused a lot of damage here.  Lucky he didn't hurt or kill anyone, and that we only had to kill him and not you, too.  Pay the bartender $100 for the damage.  Take Bob's gun belt off him and leave it and his Colt on the floor with yours, you won't be needin' 'em.  Pick up Bob and take him with you, you three are leavin' Sunrise, now!"

Alexander hesitated a moment, then continued, "Be sure to tell Stockett we don't 'preciate your kind and I want to talk with him when he's next in town. I don't want to see you or another Stockett hand in Sunrise until I've met with him and we come to an understandin'. You get that message to him directly."

Harold nodded that he understood and he and Lefty picked up Bob, carried him out of the Silver Chalet, retrieved their horses from the livery, tacked up, loaded and tied Bob across his saddle, and left town.

When they arrived back at their camp, they unloaded Bob, unsaddled the horses, and put them with the rest of the remuda. Harold was reluctant to confront Ed and tell him what happened in Sunrise, but he had to, and the sooner the better. Harold found Ed at the chuck wagon having a cup of coffee.

Harold said, "Ed, we're back early. Bob's dead. He started somethin' in the Silver Chalet that the marshal finished. Lefty and I are lucky to be alive."

Ed replied, "I thought you were going to control Bob and Lefty and see to it that you kept a low profile. What happened?"

"Bob started shooting up the Silver Chalet and wouldn't listen to me to stop. The only way I could've stopped him was to have killed him myself. As it was, the marshal came in and killed him. That marshal can draw and shoot faster than anyone else I've ever seen before. The deputy had Lefty and me covered with an eight-gauge. The marshal kept our Colts and gunbelts and made me pay $100 for the damage Bob done."

"You didn't turn in your Colts when you got to town like I told you?"

"No, we thought we'd feel naked without 'em."

"You thought!  You're not supposed to think when you're given a direct order!  You've created a problem for us.  You've put us in the marshal's sights."

"I guess we have, sorry.  The marshal said he wanted to meet with Mr. Stockett the next time he's in town, before any more of us hands are welcome there."

# 20

Alexander, Lacy, and I met for breakfast, as we did everyday, at the Café Madrid. Alexander and I were fully awake and aware, Lacy appeared tired and unfocused.

Alexander said to Lacy, "You look beat."

Lacy replied, "I am. I slept, but I'm still tired. I can't seem to get started. I think it's from sittin' on the train so long without any activity. Also, I had nothin' to do while I waited for Knight in Trinidad and while I waited for the train in Penance after meetin' with Dyson and Jackson. It'd been better for me if I'd ridden my horse there and back."

I said, "Maybe for you, but if you had, you'd still be on your way back from Trinidad. You certainly wouldn't have gotten back here yesterday."

"True enough," replied Lacy.

Just then, the Spaniard came to our table to take our order. We ordered the usual, fried sow belly, eggs, biscuits, and coffee. The Spaniard brought the biscuits, butter, and coffee quickly.

I tried the coffee, screwed up my face, and said, "Coffee isn't any better this morning. It's still next to the worst in Sunrise."

Alexander responded with a smile, "And, we know whose is worse, hands down."

While we waited for the rest of our breakfasts, Lacy told us about his trip. "When I got there Knight wasn't in Trinidad, he was out with the sheriff checkin' on some trouble at a ranch north of town. I had to wait two days for him to return. His deputy,

George Every, recommended a good place for me to eat, Sweet's Café, and a decent hotel next to Sweet's for me to stay. Nothin' exceptional for me to tell you about the two nights and the better part of two days I waited. No women, no amusements to speak of. I walked around the town and saw most of it. When I finally got to see Knight, he agreed to help us and be here the day we need him."

Alexander said, "Lacy, lucky for us you only had to wait two days for Knight instead of a week or more, tracking him down in the far corners of the county."

Lacy replied, "Yes, it was." He continued after a swallow of coffee, a bite of biscuit, and another swallow of coffee, "I met with Dyson and Jackson right after I arrived in Penance. They agreed to help us and be here the day we need 'em, too. I had to stay overnight in Penance waitin' to catch the train back here, but I was able to stay the night in an empty cell. Dyson and Jackson were kind enough to buy my meals while I was there and not lock the cell door while I slept."

I interrupted, "Your trip was a great success!"

Alexander said, "I hope nothing comes up to delay one or all of them, but just in case, we should consider a way to handle this without 'em."

Alexander looked at us and waited for one of us to say something, but neither of us did. So Alexander continued, "Think about it and talk to me later if either of you has an idea."

Then Alexander looked directly at Lacy and said, "You done well. What we needed from 'em, you got 'em to agree to. We couldn't go up against that cattle outfit without their help. Thank you. It's good to know I can rely on you to get an important assignment done by yourself."

Lacy replied, "Thanks, I 'preciate that."

I broke in saying, "Lacy, you missed the fun while you was gone. Yesterday, midday, we had to settle a ruckus at the Silver Chalet. Three riders, one was shooting up the place, the other two was standing guard just waiting for someone to challenge 'em. Trouble is, the three fellows who made the ruckus came from the cattle outfit we're preparing to deal with. Alexander killed the shooter while I held the other two off with my eight-gauge. Alexander sent 'em back to their outfit with the dead one tied across his saddle and their Colts and gun belts locked up in the marshal's office. Alexander made 'em pay $100 for the damage they caused and told 'em their whole outfit wasn't welcome in town until their boss came here and spoke with him. That 'bout right, Alexander?"

Alexander nodded his agreement. He was about to speak, but the Spaniard arrived with a big tray loaded with our breakfasts. He put our plates down on the table in front of us, bowed slightly, and left. He came back with another pot of coffee, refilled our cups, bowed again, and left us to our food.

When his breakfast was mostly gone, Alexander said, "Remember Bird was goin' to the Chiricahua res and bring back five braves to help us. By my figurin', he should be back six days from today. You agree?"

Lacy replied, "I believe you're correct."

Alexander finished his breakfast then said, "I'm sure Bird and his five Chiricahua braves'll do a fine job, but I'm not sure if they'll be able to leave the herd and the crew alone while they're doin' it. I think they may tip our hand without some guidance."

I said, "Could be," I said. "They may try to collect Bird's missin' cattle and a few scalps up front and ruin the surprise. What do you think we should do?"

Alexander continued, "I think one of us needs to be at the Runnin' Bird when Bird and the Chiricahua arrive, stay with 'em, and direct their activities. I think you, Emmett, are the right person for this because of your cavalry officer experience leading men and your experience with Indians. Will you do it?"

I replied, "Of course, what needs to be done is reconnaissance. The Chiricahua should look for cattle with brands other than Bar CS or fresh Bar CS brands run over other brands. They should also reconnoiter the valley. We need to know everything about their camps, where their chuck wagon is, where they eat, where their remuda is, where they bunch their cattle, how many bunches there are, and where they water. We need this information to develop a plan to capture, not kill, the rustlers without stampedin' the herd. Sound 'bout right, Alexander?"

Alexander nodded in agreement and said, "Sounds good to me. When'll you leave?"

I thought about it and said, "I'll leave 'bout noon, five days from today. I need to be there the day before they arrive so I have time to look over the Bar CS valley and confirm my plan. Also, I want to make sure they don't arrive at the Runnin' Bird early and start without me."

Alexander brought us back to the present. He said, "Lacy, you make mornin' town rounds. Emmett, you make afternoon town rounds. I'm goin' home for the day. I'll meet you both at the Chicago House at five for dinner. I'll make evenin' town rounds. You fellers can tag along with me for evenin' town rounds, if'n you've got no other plans. Always enjoy your company. I'm goin' home."

Alexander motioned to the Spaniard, who came quickly to our table. Alexander paid for breakfast and left for home without saying another word. I left for the Chicago House to find Jewel Marion, hoping to pass the morning with her, Lacy left for the marshal's office and to make morning town rounds.

# 21

Alexander slowly walked the short distance from the Café Madrid to his house. He was anxious about Ella. She hadn't been home for four days and nights, since just after she, Sabrina, and he had met and spoken on the street with Emmett. He didn't understand why she wasn't there for him, with him, waiting for him.

This had happened four times before. The first was when she'd taken up with a hired gun passing through Sunrise several years ago. The second was a year later when she'd taken up with a rancher who owned the Sleeping L at the time. The third was when she had run off after I'd killed the rancher for taken up with her. And, the fourth was soon after we rescued her from the whorehouse in Marfa where she'd taken up with a preacher.

Though Ella had explained why she'd taken up with the hired gun, why she'd taken up with the rancher, why she'd run off, why she'd gone back to whoring, and why she'd taken up with the preacher, Alexander hadn't understood, and still didn't. But, he felt he'd have to confront her and get this settled or he would become like the appaloosa stallion, trying to control access to a mare who would always be attracted to the dominant male. The one who would support her and provide her the status she expected. And, he knew that sooner or later it was going to be permanent and someone other than him, because he was either dead or unable to provide for her.

When he reached his house, Alexander looked for her through each of the rooms, kitchen, parlor, and both bedrooms. The house was dark, the drapes and curtains were closed and the bed was made and cold. Ella wasn't and hadn't been home.

He found his jug, took it and a glass out onto the porch, and sat. He poured a half-glass of whiskey and took a swallow, then several more, waiting for insight. It finally dawned on him that she would be at Bellas, and since she hadn't been home, she may not be coming back. He would have to go there if he wanted to talk with her. It would be difficult for him, he would rather face death than have this conversation, but he'd have to do it.

Alexander never showed emotion. He was always stoic and reserved. Though he smiled and even laughed on occasion, he never opened up and told anyone how he felt. And, he rarely carried his share of a conversation. He dreaded what he had to do, but he finished his whiskey, returned the jug and glass to the kitchen, straightened his jacket and pistol belt, put on his hat, and left for Bellas.

When he arrived there, the door opened as he raised his hand to knock. A pretty, young woman had opened it and was standing in the doorway smiling at him.

She said, "Hello marshal. We were expectin' you, though we'd figured you'd abeen here long before now. I'm sure you came to see Sabrina or Ella. They're both with clients at the moment, but they'll be finished soon. I'm Kati Madri. How may I entertain you?"

He wanted to yell, "I'm here to see Ella! Go get her immediately!" But instead he said simply, "I've come to see Ella. Where can I wait?"

Kati said, "Of course, marshal, this way." She led Alexander to the parlor and motioned for him to sit on an overstuffed sofa. She continued, "Now marshal, how may I entertain you?"

"I'd surely 'preciate a glass of whiskey."

"Certainly, marshal," Kati said with a smile and left the room. She returned with a shot glass of whiskey and set it carefully on the table next to him. She continued, "How may I further entertain you?"

"Thank you. You've been very kind, but this here's enough. Leave me now, I'd prefer to wait alone."

Kati had hoped Alexander would show an interest in going to a bedroom with her, but as she waited, it became obvious he wouldn't. So, she left him alone as he'd requested.

About thirty minutes later Ella entered the parlor and was surprised to find Alexander sleeping on the sofa. She sat next to him and tried to gently awaken him, but he came fully awake with a start pulling his Colt as he stood.

Ella said softly, "Alexander, it's OK. It's me, Ella. Put up your Colt and sit down."

Alexander looked around the room, holstered his Colt, sat down, and said, "I must have dozed. I hope I didn't upset you coming awake like that."

"Alexander, I've seen you do that more times than I care to remember. It doesn't bother me anymore, but someday you'll kill someone doing that. Alexander, why are you here?"

"You haven't been home for days. I've been worried about you. Where've you been? Here? Are you coming home?"

"Alexander, I've been right here. I told you I was going to be here. This is my home now. You should've come here to see me before now."

"Ella," Alexander said with a grimace, "I've been rescuin' you from whorehouses, bad men, and unpleasant situations for years, and you keep runnin' off. Why? Isn't our life together enough for you?"

"Alexander, I'm so happy you've finally decided to talk to me about this. I've been wantin' to for such a long time, but I didn't know how to start."

"Now's your chance."

"Yes, now's my chance and I'll not lose it. Alexander, I've got nothin', no money, no property, no position, no respect, nothing. You've no money, but you've got your house, you're the marshal, and people respect you because you're the marshal and the best shooter around. We could've had the best ranch in these parts, been married, and been rich and respected, but you won't marry me and you gave the ranch away to that Mexican half-breed. With you, I'll always be just the marshal's whore."

"No, you won't, and I don't treat you that way."

"You don't think so, but you do. Other people see how badly you treat me and they treat me just as badly. We're not married and never will be. We have no common friends except your deputies, Emmett and Lacy, and we don't go out in public together. It's either you or me, never us."

She paused, gained her strength, and continued, "If you were killed, went somewhere else, or told me to leave, I'd be alone again with nothin' and frightened more than ever. I'd have to find a way to support myself. I'd have to go to a saloon and be a whore or find a wealthy, powerful man to take care of me, which is being just another kind of whore, the kind I've been with you. And, I'd be competin' with girls younger and prettier than me. Sabrina has given me a new start, half of Bellas, half of this house and everything in it. I own somethin' here. I may be a whore, but I've got property, income, and status. I'm not comin' back to you. You can come visit me here anytime you like. Now, if you'll excuse me, I have clients to attend. I think you can find your way out. Goodbye."

Ella got up and left Alexander sitting alone in the parlor. Alexander remained seated. He was shocked, dazed, and angered by what Ella had said to him. After a few minutes, he stood and walked out of Bellas.

He turned left when he reached the street and left again at Main Street. He soon arrived at City Hall and went into the marshal's office where he sat at his desk and stared through the window at the street. He wasn't focusing on anything in particular. He kept hearing Ella saying goodbye.

I made it to the marshal's office in the late afternoon, after finishing midday town rounds. Alexander was sitting at his desk staring blankly out the window, looking crumpled in upon himself. Lacy was sitting at the other desk watching Alexander.

I said, "Afternoon."

"Afternoon," replied Lacy.

Alexander didn't say anything. He didn't seem to have heard me.

I said to Lacy, "You been here long?"

"'Bout an hour. I finished mornin' town rounds, ate lunch, had a bath and a nap, and come here."

"Alexander been like that the whole time you've been here?"

"Yes, hasn't moved or said a word. It's been quiet in town, nothin' seems to be happenin' and nobody's come to the office. However, somethin' must've happened or be terribly wrong for Alexander to be actin' this way. I've never seen him like this. I bet he's been to Bellas and talked with Ella."

"You're probably right. Let's take him to dinner and then home. You and I can do evenin' town rounds without him."

# 22

The next morning, Lacy and I met early at the Marshal's Office. We had hoped to find Alexander already there waiting for us and learn what was bothering him, but he wasn't. We waited a while then walked to his house and knocked on the front door. Alexander didn't answer. We knocked louder and made lots of noise stomping our feet and calling his name.

He finally opened the door. He was fully dressed, ready for the street, wearing his jacket, hat, and gun belt. And, he was glaring at us with a frown on his face that would have killed lesser men. Lacy and I backed down the stairs off of the porch.

He said with a hint of anger in his voice, "Why all this ruckus?"

Lacy replied, "It's time for breakfast. You know the Spaniard, he'll run out of eggs if we don't get there pretty quick. How about let's get a move on."

Alexander continued to stand in the doorway glaring at us. He finally nodded, stepped out of the house, shut the door, joined us at the bottom of the stairs, and led the way to the Café Madrid.

While we were eating breakfast, we saw Harold from the Bar CS ride by on Main Street in front of the restaurant with two other men. By the way the other two were dressed and the quality of the horses they were riding, one had to be the foreman, and the other, the owner of the Bar CS, the two men we had seen in the Chicago House a while back.

Alexander, Lacy, and I watched the men as they rode to the livery. A short while later we saw them leave the livery and walk toward the Chicago House.

"Looks like they're goin' to the Chicago House. I think we've eaten enough," Alexander growled. "Let's go join 'em at the Chicago House. I've a bone to pick with 'em about Harold's last visit. We need to make sure Bar CS riders follow town rules. And, we need to know what they have in mind about settlin' in that valley, keepin' a large herd, and bein' good neighbors."

Alexander motioned for the check and paid the Spaniard. We rose from our chairs and left for the Chicago House. When we arrived there, we passed through the batwing doors going in different directions when inside. Lacy went left with his Colt out, held straight out in front of him pointing at the Bar CS riders. He stood very still, slightly crouched. I went right with my eight-gauge held loosely at my shoulder, pointed at the Bar CS riders. I also stood very still, slightly crouched. Alexander went straight up the middle of the room. He brushed his coat back from his holstered Colt, kept his hands at his sides, and walked directly to the table occupied by the three Bar CS riders.

He looked from one to the other and said, "Welcome to Sunrise. I recognize Harold, but you two I don't remember seein' before. All three of you are wearin' gun belts. Harold should have told you our rules. You have to turn in all guns, gun belts, and knives at the sheriff's office or here to Clay, the bartender, as soon as you get to town. You can have them back when you leave. Now, all three of you are goin' to slowly stand, unbuckle your gun belts, hold them by their buckles, and one at a time, walk over to the bar and give them belts to Clay and return immediately to this table. You'll do this real slow. Any fast moves or if you don't exactly follow my instructions, my two deputies would like nothing better than to put you down. Harold, I'll put you down myself. So, you first, move."

They didn't move. They sat and looked at each other, weighing their chances if they were to draw on us and silently asking each other what to do. Their bravado died as quickly as it blossomed, and they pushed back their chairs, stood, and followed Alexander's instructions.

After all three had given their Colts and gun belts to Clay and had returned to their table and were back in their chairs, Alexander sat down at their table and loudly said, "Clay, a glass and a bottle of your good whisky. I won't drink the whisky you served these fellows. Bring Emmett and Lacy each a beer."

Clay nodded in response and went about drawing the beer and fetching a bottle and a glass for Alexander. No-one said anything. All six of us waited while Clay served.

Alexander said, "Two of you I don't already know, though I remember seein' you in here a while ago. You'd best introduce yourselves and describe your relationship to Harold."

The older of the two men spoke first, "I'm Charles Stockett. I own the Bar CS. I recently sold my ranch near Murphyville, Texas. My foreman, my hands, and I drove my herd to a valley near here. We stopped there because that valley looks perfect for our needs. I intend to settle there permanently."

The other man spoke next, "I'm Ed Vargas, Mr. Stockett's foreman. I've been his foreman for several years and have helped grow his herd and his ranch."

Harold was last, "I'm Harold. I'm one of Mr. Stockett's scouts. I and four other scouts blazed trail and pointed for the herd all the way here from Murphyville."

Alexander thought for a minute, then said, "Emmett and I been to Texas. We were a spell in Marfa, near Murphyville. Here in Colorado, we do things a mite different. We follow the law. We have rules. And, that includes you, now that you're here."

Alexander paused and waited for one of the Bar CS men to respond, but they remained quiet. So he continued, "While in our jurisdiction, you'll follow our rules. You can read the rules. They're posted on the wall in every saloon and on the front wall of City Hall, where the marshal's office is. The county deputy sheriff, Rawlins Knight, has deputized us to mind the law around Sunrise. So, you'd be advised to play it straight in all of your actions. Is there anythin' you need me to clarify or do you understand my meanin'?"

Stockett answered, "We understand. We don't have any quarrel with you, nor do we want one."

Alexander continued, "Now to the ruckus Harold and his two friends caused in the Silver Chalet. You've lost a hand. I had to kill him. He tried my resolve. Anyone who does will get the same by me or my two deputies, Emmett and Lacy. Do you understand?"

Stockett answered again, "We understand."

Alexander again continued, "Lastly, your three hands caused considerable damage to the Silver Chalet shootin' up the place, pissin' on the floor, and breakin' furniture. Lowell Williams, the owner, says it amounted to $100. Harold paid that, but it'll cost you much more than that next time."

Stockett said, "I'll control my hands and make sure it doesn't happen again. Can my hands now come into Sunrise?"

Alexander answered, "Yes, they can. I think we're through here. Good day."

Alexander stood up from the table, turned, and walked out of the Chicago House the same way he entered, straight to and through the batwing doors. Lacy holstered his pistol and followed Alexander out of the saloon. I hesitated a second, lowered the hammers on both barrels of my eight-gauge, and followed them outside.

We regrouped in the street in front of the Chicago House. Alexander said to us, "I'm goin' to the marshal's office. The marshal should be in his office from time-to-time. You two do mornin' town rounds. Be sure to visit both the small merchants and the saloons this mornin'. Spend extra time with each of the small merchants. Chat 'em up. Make 'em feel they're important. After all, they pay part of our salaries and don't get much attention. When you're done, meet me at the marshal's office and we'll go to lunch. I'm thinkin' we've been lunch and dinner guests of Ward Layne at the Chicago House quite regular. I think we should be lunch and dinner guests of Lowell Williams at the Silver Chalet today. Any disagreement?"

None was forthcoming. Without another word, Alexander crossed the street and walked off toward the marshal's office. We watched him as he crossed the street, then we walked off in the opposite direction, but staying on the same side of the street as the Chicago House.

Charles, Ed, and Harold relaxed after they were alone, though they were visibly shaken from their encounter with Alexander. They had feared for their lives. Charles and Ed were not known to fight unless the odds were in their favor. And in this situation, although it had been three against three, the odds had been decidedly lopsidedly in favor of the marshal and his two deputies.

Charles said, "Let's have dinner here then go to Bellas for the evenin' and stay the night. Harold, I think you'll find Bellas to your liking. I'll be with Sabrina. Ed you'll be with Ella. And, Harold, you'll be with Kati."

Charles looked at Ed then Harold. Seeing no disagreement, he continued, "We'll go to the Café Madrid for breakfast early tomorrow mornin'. After breakfast, Harold, you pick up an escort or freight wagon and four-horse team from the livery and meet Ed and me at the mercantile to purchase supplies."

Harold replied, "Why don't we go get one of our own wagons?"

Ed answered, "We'd loose two days fetching it and returning."

Charles continued, "We three will load the wagon ourselves and leave together for the Bar CS. Harold, you'll drive the wagon. I don't want to stay here tomorrow any longer than necessary. Harold, you'll return the wagon and team to the livery the day after tomorrow. And, Ed, send two hands with Harold to return the wagon and team to the livery to make sure he has a safe trip."

Ed and Harold nodded.

Ed said, "Charles, don't forget, we have to stop here on our way out of town to pick up our guns."

Harold said, "On the way to Bellas, I'll stop at the livery and reserve a wagon and team for early tomorrow morning."

# 23

Charles, Ed, and Harold awakened just after sunrise and found themselves alone in unfamiliar beds. They struggled up, wobbled to their feet, dressed, and carefully made their way to Bellas' kitchen, hungover and feeling miserable. They took seats around the kitchen table.

Kati was already in the kitchen. She had prepared coffee for them. As she filled their cups, she received grunts of thanks. The strong coffee woke them up and started clearing their heads. They slowly felt life returning.

Sabrina and Ella came into the kitchen together. Sabrina said, "Thank you boys for visitin' us. We surely do 'preciate your visit and our time together, but it's time for us to prepare for a new day. We have to make ourselves and this place presentable. It's time for you to be on your way."

They hadn't planned on leaving so early in the morning, but accepted being turned out, and said goodbye. On their way to the front door they were met by Gerald Kroutsch, who escorted them out and locked the door behind them.

They went to the Café Madrid for breakfast. When they finished and were back on the street, Harold said, "I'll get the freight wagon and team from the livery and meet you at the mercantile."

Charles and Ed nodded and headed up Main Street to the mercantile. As they entered, Charles pulled a folded paper from his pocket, their shopping list.

Charles said, "I'll see to foodstuffs, you see to hardware, fencin', and guns and ammunition."

Ed nodded.

"By hardware, I mean nails, fence staples, and tools. We didn't bring any fencin' tools with us. We need hammers, wire stretchers, and wire cutters. Enough tools for two fencin' crews. And, a couple of hand saws and a two-man saw to cut planks, beams, and posts."

"I understand."

"For fencin', only get a dozen 440-yard rolls of barbed wire today, that's enough to three-strand a quarter section. Have three dozen more rolls put aside for us so we can fence another three quarter sections before fall. We'll pick up the additional barbed wire after we finish the first quarter section."

"Alright."

"And be sure you get enough fencin' staples for the full section. We'll take enough today for the first quarter section. Don't forget we'll need a couple of shovels to dig post holes."

"I've got it."

"What do you think 'bout guns and ammunition?"

Ed thought for a bit and then replied, "I think we should standardize on the Colt Single Action Army revolver Model 1878, chambered for the Winchester .44-40 Winchester Center Fire cartridge and the Winchester lever action rifle that fires the same cartridge. A dozen of each, one each for you and me, and one each for the hands that don't have weapons. That'll leave us with a couple spares. Colts and Winchesters."

"That's reasonable, I agree." Charles said.

"And, lastly, a case of cartridges. Will give one box each to you and me and to each of the hands we've given weapons to. We'll store the rest for when the shootin' starts."

"OK."

Ed nodded, and they both moved off to see to their purchases.

Harold arrived with the wagon and team at the back of the mercantile just as the store owner and his clerk began stacking the Bar CS purchases there. The size of the stack amazed Harold as it grew larger. When the store owner and his clerk finished, there were several sacks of flour, sugar, corn, and beans, a dozen rolls of barbed wire, a case of nails and one of fence staples, a case of Colt revolvers, a case of Winchester rifles, a case of Winchester .44-40 cartridges, a couple of hammers, fence stretchers, and fence cutters, a two-man saw, and a couple of shovels.

Harold saw that their purchases would have to be taken in two loads, there was just too much for one. He decided what should be taken in each load and calculated the weight of each load to make sure the wagon would carry it and the team could pull it.

When he felt comfortable with his loading plan, he went into the mercantile looking for Charles and Ed. He found them at the front counter with the owner drinking lemonade and eating fresh pastries. The owner offered Harold a glass of lemonade and a pastry, which he gladly accepted.

Harold said to Charles and Ed, "I looked at your purchases stacked out back. There's so much it'll have to be taken in two trips. I've planned what goes in each."

Ed said, "Explain."

Harold replied, "The first load should be the foodstuffs, guns, and ammunition. The second load should be the barbed wire, nails, staples, and tools. I'll take the first load today, return tomorrow, and return to the ranch with the second load the day after tomorrow. I'll return the freight wagon and team to the livery the day after. Wagon team can only go one direction in a day. I'll need two hands for three days to help me."

"OK," Ed said. "Let's load up and get on our way."

When they finished loading the wagon, they walked to the livery, saddled their horses, mounted, and rode back to the mercantile. Harold put a halter and lead rope on his horse and handed the lead to Ed. Harold climbed up onto the wagon's bench, released the brake, and set the team in motion. They left Sunrise to the north, on the road to Penance. When the road forked, they took the track to the east. There was another fork further on, the north track went to the Running Bird, the other track went east toward their valley and continued eastward into Kansas. They took the east track.

When they arrived at their camp, Ed said, "Harold, leave the wagon and team in front of the storage tent, go get somethin' to eat, and go to bed. You've got three more days of this."

Harold nodded and went to care for his horse, eat, and turn in.

Ed called to the wrangler and three hands to come over. He said to the hands, "Unload the wagon. Put the foodstuffs in the storage tent and the guns and ammunition in mine."

To the wrangler Ed added, "After they're finished unloadin', unhitch the team and see that each of 'em gets a good rubdown, plenty to eat, and fresh water to drink. They're gonna be used hard over the next three days. Keep 'em separated from our remuda. They aren't ours. They belong to the livery in Sunrise."

He dismissed the four of them by saying, "Get movin', it's goin' to be dark soon."

# 24

It was an hour after sunrise and Alexander, Lacy, and I were having breakfast at the Café Madrid, as we did almost every morning. Since I was to leave this morning for the Running Bird where I was to meet Bird and five Chiricahua he was bring back with him from the res, Alexander wanted to make sure I understood what I was to do while there and what I was to learn about the Bar CS.

Alexander said, "Emmett, you ready to go?"

I replied, slightly upset by his question, "As ready as I'll ever be. I've got a bedroll, clothes, coat, slicker, gun belt, Colt, Winchester, and eight-gauge, ammunition for all three, and a great dislike for rustlers. Can you think of anythin' else I might need?"

Alexander smiled, "I know you can put a travel kit together and I know you don't like rustlers. It's the plan for what you're goin' to do once you're there that I want to hear."

I thought for a bit before I responded, "Well, I thought I'd start by packing my kit right after breakfast and help with mornin' town rounds after that. I'll leave for the Runnin' Bird after we complete mornin' town rounds and have lunch."

Alexander nodded.

"I should arrive at the Runnin' Bird middle of the afternoon. Once there, I thought I'd take a look over the ridge to the east and get a feelin' for the layout of the Bar CS, see how their herd is spread out and how they're workin' it. That will allow me to plan how Bird and the Chiricahua will reconnoiter."

"Good so far. Give me specifics."

"Can't, yet, not until I'm there and see the layout. My basic goals are to learn how big their herd is, how their herd is spread across the valley, how many hands they have, if the their brand is on all the cattle, are any of the brands run, and if so, what were the original brands."

"Alright, but remember Bird and the Chiricahua are to reconnoiter not encounter. They're not to be seen or heard. They're not to approach. Bird and the Chiricahua are to gather information not confront the Bar CS crew in any way."

"Yes, you've said that before and I understand and agree."

"Sorry if I've offended you by pushing these things, but you're the key to this operation and I don't want any misunderstandings. I guess I'll just have to trust you and await developments."

Alexander and I smiled at that.

Alexander continued, "You know there were Bar CS hands in and out of town the past few days. Three days ago they got a wagon and team from the livery, loaded the wagon full of foodstuffs and weapons from the mercantile, and drove the load out of town. Probably to their ranch. Two days ago, they returned with the wagon. Yesterday, they loaded the wagon full of barbed wire and tools from the mercantile, and drove their second load out of town. Probably also to their ranch. They may return today for another load or to return the wagon and team. You may meet 'em on the road as they're comin' into or leavin' town. Don't let on 'bout where you're going or what you're up to. Don't ride with 'em or let 'em know where you're goin'."

I replied, "I understand."

We finished breakfast, Alexander paid, as usual, and we walked out of the Café Madrid to the street. We stopped. Alexander and I nodded to each other. Alexander and Lacy moved off toward the marshal's office in City Hall. I left for the Chicago House.

About an hour later, I arrived at the marshal's office fresh from a bath and shave. I was wearing a clean set of clothes and carrying my eight-gauge and a warm coat wrapped in a slicker in one hand and my Winchester and saddle bags, bulging with clothes, an extra revolver and ammunition in the other. And, I had my bedroll and a canteen full of fresh water slung over my shoulder.

I nodded to Lacy as I entered and said, "I need to drop this stuff at the livery then how 'bout you and me doin' mornin' town rounds?"

Lacy nodded.

To Alexander I said, "We'll meet you at the Chicago House for lunch in 'bout an hour?"

Alexander didn't look up, but nodded.

Lacy stood up and we left the marshal's office for the livery together. Morning town rounds went smoothly and slowly. Nothing of note was happening anywhere in town. We took our time paying our respects to shop owners and saloon keepers, making sure they felt they were important to us. We met Alexander for lunch.

After lunch, I walked to the livery, brushed my horse, cleaned his feet, tacked up, tied my saddle bags, bedroll, and slicker wrapped coat over the saddle's rear skirt, put my Winchester in its scabbard, and looped my canteen over the saddle horn. I was ready. I led my horse out of the barn, and mounted up..

As I rode out of the livery, I passed the Bar CS hands, Harold and two others, as they were bringing back the wagon and team. Harold nodded at me and I nodded back. The other two Bar CS hands looked at me with indifference.

I pressed my calves against my horse's lower sides, pushing him into a jog trot and took the north road out of Sunrise toward Penance. About an hour later, just as I took the east fork toward the Running Bird, the Bar CS hands overtook me at a lope, and we all stopped in the middle of the track.

Harold said, "Afternoon Emmett."

I nodded in response.

Harold said, "Goin' visiting?"

"No, just out breezing my mount and taking a couple of days out of town."

"You're carryin' a lot of stuff, slicker, eight-gauge, Winchester, and full saddle bags. You must be plannin' to stay a while, or maybe you're leavin' town for good?"

"You seem very interested in my doin's."

"No special interest and no disrespect intended, just bein' neighborly. Do you mind if we ride along with you a spell?"

"Not at all. I'm planning to ride up into the hills over yonder. You gonna join me?"

"No, don't think so. We got to get back to the Bar CS. I guess we'll be on our way." They left pushing their horses into a lope.

I remained stopped in the track until they had disappeared in their own dust, then I pushed my horse back into a jog trot and continued riding toward the east following after them. When I came to the next fork, I went to the north and eventually came into the valley just west of the Running Bird and saw the gray leopard appaloosa stallion and his mares on the other side. The stallion picked up his head, flared his nostrils, and snorted. I reined to a stop and watched him come between me and his mares, motioning by throwing his head that he didn't welcome me there and challenging me. I smiled, amused by his behavior. I didn't want to disturb them any more than necessary, so, as usual, I rode the crest of the hill around the edge of the valley, and dropped off the crest on the other side down to the Running Bird.

As I rode up to the bunkhouse and dismounted, Claire came running out of the barn excitedly waving her arms in greeting. When she reached me she jumped into my arms and held tight. Following behind her at a walk and far less excited was John Fields. When Claire released me and moved away, John Fields nodded at me in greeting.

I pointed to the bunkhouse and said to John, "Is that where I'm to bed down?"

"Yes. Put your stuff on any empty bunk. I see you brought a bedroll. I'll bring you a blanket some time before dinner. It's getting might chilly these evenin's," John replied.

"Thank you," I replied.

Claire said, "Freshen up and come to the house for dinner."

I said, "I'll put my stuff in the bunkhouse. Then I'm goin' up on the ridge to the east to look over the Bar CS. I'll be back for dinner after sunset. Is that alright?"

Claire replied, "Yes, of course. I'll have dinner ready for you."

# 25

I went into the bunkhouse, dropped my bedroll, slicker wrapped coat, and saddle bags on an empty bunk, and returned to my horse. I checked my cinch and the rest of my tack, mounted, and rode out the gate behind the barn up the hill into the pines. I stayed among the pines for cover as I slowly climbed, stopping every so often to check if I was alone.

After about a mile, I reached the crest of the hill, dismounted near a large pile of boulders, and tethered my horse to a chest-high branch of a nearby, sturdy pine. The base of the boulder pile was roughly square, about 60 feet on a side. There were large boulders on the bottom, smaller ones nearer the top, and a scattering of small rocks and pebbles on and between them. Altogether, the pile was maybe 20 feet tall. I carefully climbed to the top of the pile. From there, I could clearly see the whole valley. There weren't any trees inhibiting the view east from the top of the boulder pile.

I took Alexander's spyglass from my pocket and slowly scanned the valley. I started from my left, the north side of the valley, looking for cattle. They were scattered mostly around the middle of the valley. There were some loners, some groups of two or three, several bunches of between 20 and 50, and two herds of what appeared to be close to 1,000 each. I figured the total was close to 2,500 head. There was a wide, shallow, free flowing river passing from north to south straight through the center of the valley. A large number of cattle were in the river along its banks, on its banks, and within 150 feet of its banks.

Near the center of the valley, just to the east of the river, was what seemed to be the ranch headquarters. There was a chuck wagon, a fire pit with two concentric rings of logs circling it, and 16 tents just beyond the outside ring on the opposite side of the rings of logs from the chuck wagon..

There were three sizes of tents, a large one that could be storage, two medium ones, probably living accommodations for Stockett and Vargas, and thirteen smaller ones. The smaller ones were surely for the crew. Each of the smaller ones appeared to be large enough for two men. One of the smaller tents was separate from the others, close to the front of the chuck wagon. That one was certainly for the cook and his helper, if he had one.

The number of tents implied there could be between 15 and 28 men. The actual number depended upon how many of the smaller tents were occupied by one or two men.

Off to the side and some distance from the tents was a trench partially enclosed with canvass nailed to posts buried in the ground, the latrine. Beyond the latrine was a roped off area with the remuda peacefully grazing within it.

I scanned the valley starting from my left again, this time looking for men, either on foot or horseback. I knew I wouldn't get an exact count, it would be difficult to distinguish men on foot or on horseback from the cattle they were herding, especially this late in the afternoon, but I could come reasonably close. I saw two riders at the edge of the valley, three riders among the small bunches of cattle, and three riders around the outside edge of each of the two herds. I had identified 11 riders, adding the owner, the foreman, and the cook and his helper, a total of 15 men. There may be one or more sleeping, the night crew, so I had accounted for 16 or more men. I continued looking.

In the distance, against the north hills of the valley, there were three small cabins that appeared to be about one-half mile apart. Each cabin had at least one outbuilding and corrals. These must be the small ranches the Bar CS took over when they moved into the valley. An army escort wagon was next to the middle cabin, a about a dozen horses were in its three corrals, four to a corral, and smoke was rising from its chimney. Eight of the horses were probably two four-horse wagon teams, the other three horses were smaller, probably riding horses. This could signify three men, each with one riding horse, or two men with an extra riding horse each. The number of crew I had identified had grown, it was now between 18 and 20 men.

I heard movement nearby. I stopped looking into the valley, quietly closed Alexander's spyglass, and deftly put it back in my pocket. I concentrated on listening and watching at where I thought the sound had come. I didn't have long to wait, a man carrying a saddle gun briefly came into view sliding between the pines just a few feet away from the boulder pile.

He was slowly and quietly moving between trees. He'd move to a tree, stop behind it, look and listen a while, and move to another tree. I was certain he was looking for me. I climbed down the boulder pile to the ground, careful not to dislodge any of the small rocks or pebbles, keeping an eye on him all the way down. I drew my Colt, crept up behind him, and pushed the end of the Colt's barrel hard into the center of his back.

I said commandingly, "Stop. Drop the saddle gun."

He started to spin around lifting his rifle as he turned. I hit him hard on the side of the head, just above the ear, with the barrel of my Colt. He dropped his saddle gun and fell forward onto his chest, face in the dirt. I thought I'd knocked him out or maybe even killed him, but he surprised me by flipping over onto his back, partially sitting up, and going for his Colt. He didn't have a chance. My Colt was already in my hand and pointed squarely at him. I shot him once in the middle of the chest. He flew backward, spread eagled in the dirt. He was dead before the back of his head hit the ground.

Now I had a problem. I couldn't leave his body up here on the ridge in case other Bar CS hands came looking for him. I would have to take his body down to the Running Bird and bury it and his personals there where they wouldn't be easily found. I would also have to dispose of his horse. A Bar CS hand may recognize it. I decided to give the horse to Bird to hide in his remuda. Though, first I had to find it.

He wouldn't have walked far from his horse, it should be somewhere close. I walked to where I had left my horse and began looking for his. I found it tied to a tree a short distance away. I untied it, led it close to where his body lay, and tied it to another tree. I spoke quietly and soothingly to the horse as I lifted the dead body and tied it securely across his saddle. I picked up the saddle gun and put it in it's scabbard, led the horse to where I had left mine, untied my horse, mounted, and rode through the trees leading the other horse and the dead body down the hill to the Running Bird.

As I reined to a stop in front of the barn, John Fields met me and took the reins of the dead man's horse. I dismounted. John asked no questions. He called over two hands and told them to bury the dead man and all his personals where they wouldn't be easily found and return with the horse and turn it loose in with the remuda.

The hands led the horse with the dead body still tied in the saddle into the trees behind the barn. I was certain they would take his Colt and saddle gun, his ammunition, and anything else of value they found. They were welcome to all of it.

I led my horse into the barn, put him in a stall, took off my tack, brushed him well, and gave him a bucket of water and a large armful of hay. Then I went to the bunkhouse to freshen up before going to the ranch house for dinner. I had developed quite an appetite.

# 26

I woke early. I appeared to be the only one awake. Inside the bunkhouse, it was quiet and very dark, almost black. Outside, the sky was clear and just as dark. What little light there was outside came from the twinkling of thousands of stars.

I unwrapped myself from my bedroll and the blanket John Fields had left for me, stood up, and dressed, pants, socks, boots, and gun belt. I went outside at the north end of the bunkhouse carrying my eight-gauge and a shirt. I put my eight-gauge down, leaned it against the wall, and hung my shirt on a nail. On the shelf attached to the side of the bunkhouse were a tin water pitcher, a tin bowl and a couple bars of homemade soap. I poured water from the water pitcher into the bowl and washed and rinsed my chest, neck, arms, hands, and face. I combed my hair with wet fingers. I dried with the towel I found hanging from another nail, hung the towel back up, and put on my shirt. It was just beginning to lighten at the horizon to the east.

I picked up my eight-gauge and walked around to the south side of the bunkhouse. The kitchen windows were lit and terrific smells were wafting out from them. Breakfast for the hands was being cooked. I heard the sound of water splashing nearby with the cadence of a person walking. Someone was obviously fetching water. Another person was laying the table on the porch on the east side of the bunkhouse. I could hear people at the barn feeding and watering horses. I assumed whoever was feeding and watering at the barn would feed and water my horse with all the others.

These were the beginnings of the normal daily ranch routine. I was fortunate to be here to experience and enjoy them before they were disrupted by the arrival of a bunch of strangers and the coming fight with the Bar CS.

I climbed onto the porch and became part of the breakfast crowd. I found an empty space on the bench at the near side of the table and squeezed in, placing the butt of my eight-gauge on the floor with the barrel running up along my right side. I was greeted by John Fields and several of the hands. I felt very much at home and comfortable with these men.

The table was set with enough food for an army. I could tell you weren't expected to stand on ceremony at breakfast. You had to dig right in before the food was gone, and it was disappearing quickly. So, I did. I filled my plate with eggs, meat, potatoes, a slab of bread, and some butter. And, most importantly, filled my cup with coffee that smelled good and strong.

There were a few grunts and requests to pass a platter of food, but not much conversation. When everyone's initial hunger seemed sated and they started to slow down, John Fields stood up and gave the day's assignments. The assignments seemed fair, not a single hand complained about his or asked for a change. One by one they excused themselves from the table, taking their plates, cups, and flatware and placing them in the appropriate bucket of warm water to the side of the kitchen door. From there they scattered to begin their assignments.

My plan for the day was to meet with Bird and the Chiricahua he was bringing back from the res and plan how they would reconnoiter the Bar CS over the next few days. Since, I didn't know what time they'd arrive, some time between now and sunset, I needed to find activities to fill my day.

I decided on three. First, clean and oil my guns, Colt revolver, Winchester carbine, and eight-gauge shotgun. Second, clean my tack, saddle, breast collar, cinches, bridle, reins, and saddle bags. Spread along the bottoms of my saddle bags I carry gun and tack cleaning materials, a cleaning rag, a bar of soap, a small bottle of mineral oil, and a tin of saddle soap. Third, tour the heart of the ranch, become familiar with its buildings, corrals, fences, topography, and cover in case the fight with the Bar CS came here to the Running Bird.

When all hands had left the porch and the table had been cleaned, I went into the bunkhouse, collected my cleaning materials, and returned to the porch with my guns to clean and oil them. I had done this task so often I could accomplish it quickly wearing a blindfold, since my life depended upon my guns performing perfectly, every time. It didn't pay to be quick at this task, it was important to be thorough. When I finished with my guns and put them up, it was time to do my tack. I went to the barn, collected my tack from where it was hanging on a saddle rack on the inside wall of the barn, and carried it outside. I hung my tack on the hitching rack, and piece by piece, cleaned it. When I finished, I returned my tack to the same saddle rack on the inside wall of the barn.

Next was the ranch tour. I started by walking to the barbed wire fence behind the barn, turned right, and walked along the fence. The fence completely encircled the heart of the ranch in the form of a large rectangle. The layout within the fence was the main house to the south, the barns and out buildings to the north and east, and the bunkhouse in between, at the center. The corrals were in the northwest corner and took up nearly a quarter of the fenced area. There was a wide wooden main gate in the fence to the west and smaller wooden gates in the fence to the north, east, and south.

It was a bit past lunch time when Claire found me returning to the bunkhouse. She said, "You weren't here for lunch. Aren't you hungry?"

"Yes, I am and I'm ready for a nap, too. Cleaning my guns and tack and touring the ranch was tiring and took more time than I thought they would."

"Get washed and come to the house, lunch is ready. After you've eaten, you can return to the bunkhouse and nap. Bird will come down to collect you soon after he arrives."

I came wide awake with a start. My right hand and arm were being held in a bear trap. I was sitting up on my bunk, my right arm fully extended upward in front of me, my hand in a fist. I had tried to hit the man standing next to my bunk who had awakened me, but I had not succeeded. It was Bird, smiling down at me. I smiled back and nodded, relaxing. He waited a moment, then released me.

I stood up from my bunk and went outside carrying my shirt and washed the sleep from my face and finger combed my hair. I dried with the towel I had used earlier, put on my shirt, climbed the stairs to the bunkhouse porch, and sat at the table across from Bird.

I said, "Afternoon, Bird. That was one heck of a way to wake me."

Bird responded, "You come awake violently, you need to be careful. Someone may take offense."

"I'll work on that," I replied. "How was your trip? Were you successful? Did any Chiricahua come back with you?"

"Trip was uneventful. Didn't see anyone goin', kept to myself. And, I was successful. The best five Chiricahua returned with me. We didn't see anyone returnin', kept to ourselves."

I nodded and said, "Bird, we need to discuss how we're going to approach your neighbor, the Bar CS, over the next few days. The Chiricahua should be with us for this discussion. Go round 'em up and bring 'em back here to the bunkhouse porch. I'll be waitin'."

Bird nodded, stood, and left toward the barn. I went to the bunkhouse kitchen, poured a cup of coffee, and returned to the porch to wait.

Bird came back with the Chiricahua. The six of them sat together on the other side of the table across from me.

Bird said, "These Chiricahua are from the Chokonen band, most often called Navajo. They live southwest of here in the Arizona Territory, in the mountains northeast of Flagstaff."

I nodded that I understood.

"They've taken the names of five past Chiricahua chiefs and want to be called by their names while here. Starting from my right," Bird said nodding at each as he named them, "are Mangus, Gil-lee, Taza, Loco, and Mahko."

I nodded to each one as Bird said his name. They were distinctively dressed and physically different in stature and height. I'll be able to tell them apart and remember their names.

I said, "Do any of 'em speak English or will you translate for 'em? And, if you translate, will you translate as we speak or after we're finished?"

Bird said, "They don't speak English. I'll tell 'em what we said and what we decide when we're finished and I'm alone with 'em."

I continued, "OK. Until we move against the Bar CS, they mustn't be seen by anyone except your hands and as little as possible. And, your hands need to be told not to mention to anyone that they're here."

Bird nodded that he understood.

I continued, "I'll visit the ranches to the north, west, and south and inquire about any trouble they've had with the Bar CS. I'll ask 'em if they've recently lost any cattle, and, if so, how many. I'll go every other day beginnin' tomorrow to the ranches in one direction, and return the day after. That means, tomorrow to the north, two days from now to the west, and two days after that to the south."

Bird again nodded.

I said, "The Chiricahua should go to the Bar CS and reconnoiter each of the next six days around sunrise, before the full Bar CS crew begins their daily routines. Only the night crew is with the herd at sunrise."

Bird nodded.

I continued, "There are two main herds of about 1,000 head each and many bunches of between 20 and 50. You and the Chiricahua should go to the top of the ridge this afternoon and look at the layout for yourselves. You should decide how they'll reconnoiter the two main herds and the small bunches. I want to know 'bout how many cattle they look at and how many aren't carrying the Bar CS brand, or have the Bar CS brand run over another. And, Alexander does not want 'em to approach or have any contact with the Bar CS hands. They're just gatherin' information."

Bird nodded.

I finished with, "On the days I return, after you and I discuss what I've learned, we'll discuss what you've learned. Can you do this?"

Bird answered, "Yes, Emmett, we can."

I rose from the table, nodded at them, and left.

Bird and the Chiricahua sat quietly. Bird looked at each of them and waited for each to acknowledge him before explaining in *Chishi*, the Navajo dialect of Apache, what he and I had discussed. When finished, Bird stood, lowered his head slightly, and left them. They would discuss what Bird told them and decide to either help him or return home.

Bird returned after about 30 minutes. He said to Mangus, the oldest and the one who commanded the most respect, "Father, what is your decision?"

"We will stay with you, my son," Mangus replied.

Bird was relieved, and said, "We should climb now and look into the valley while the sun is still high. We should climb on foot so we are shadows among the trees."

They rose from the table, collected their Winchesters, and silently climbed the hill behind the barn.

# 27

José had been General Love's cook and houseboy. He stayed on when Bird and Claire took over the ranch and was doing the same work for them. Tonight, he cooked a delicious dinner for us, steak, vegetables, fresh bread and butter, and plenty of coffee. I'm sure this meal was much tastier than what the hands were getting tonight, it was much better than the lunch Claire had prepared for me this afternoon. I'm also sure the lunch Claire made for me was better than anything Ella could have made. José was probably giving her cooking lessons. Someone should have given lessons to Ella.

Our dinner conversation was light. Bird told about his trip to the Chiricahua. Claire told about what happened at the ranch in Bird's absence. I told about the latest happenings in Sunrise, including Ella's new business with Sabrina White called Bellas, and that Ella was living at Bellas and Alexander was living alone in his house. Bird didn't seem overly surprised at the news about Ella, but Claire seemed to take it very hard and began crying.

She said, "Alexander and Ella brought me through the most terrible time of my life. I feel I've lost somethin' with 'em being apart and Ella back bein' a whore. That really makes me sad."

I sensed there was nothing of value I could add, so I just nodded in response.

After dinner, Bird and I excused ourselves from the table, left the house, and walked out through the gate behind the barn into the trees to visit the Chiricahua. When we neared their camp, Bird gently touched my arm signalling me to stop. He called softly to them in *Chishi*, telling them we were there. The response must have been positive because Bird touched my arm again signalling me to start walking. When we entered their camp, they were sitting around a small campfire cooking dinner. Bird nodded in greeting and they each nodded back. I copied him and received nods in return. I felt accepted.

Bird spoke with them for quite a while. He finally turned to me and said, "They went up to the ridge and looked into the valley. They saw what you saw, cattle, two large herds, many small bunches, a few singles and pairs. They saw the river through the middle of the valley, approximately 15 riders, a camp of many tents, a chuck wagon, and a remuda."

"Yes," I said. "That's what I saw."

"There's more. They saw at the widest point of the river a stand of large cottonwoods, ten trees, a stand large enough to easily hide many men."

"I either missed that stand of trees or didn't find 'em important and they didn't register. What do they have in mind?"

"Their plan is to leave here on foot several hours before dawn tomorrow so they arrive at the cottonwoods just before dawn and hide among 'em. They'll take three uncured cowhides with 'em. At dawn, three of 'em will cover themselves with the cowhides and go among the cattle that come to the river to drink. They'll look at the brands. The other two will rest and watch from their hidin' place in the trees for approachin' Bar CS hands. They'd like to use your spyglass. Those wearing cowhides will stay among the cattle until they're tired or until Bar CS hands are to close and it isn't safe to stay in the open any longer. Then they'll return to the trees and trade places with those who have been watchin'. They'll stay in the valley until after midday, when they'll return here.  They'll do this tomorrow and each of the next five days."

I thought about what Bird said and asked him to repeat it to make sure I had it straight.  He did and I thought about it some more.

Finally, I said, "OK.  It's a good plan, but what about meals?"

Bird replied, "They'll eat breakfast before they leave in the mornin'.  They'll take jerky to eat during the day.  They'll be next to the river, they'll have plenty to drink.  They'll make their own dinner after they return in the late afternoon."

I thought about this and finally said, "OK, good, but you know that Alexander will be mighty unhappy if his spyglass is lost or damaged.  He'll blame me and take it out of my hide.  Ask them to be careful with it."

Bird smiled.

I nodded to the Chiricahua and left for the bunkhouse.  I was sure Bird and the Chiricahua had last minute details to discuss and preparation to make, as did I.  They for the Chiricahua's trip into the valley and me for my trip to the four ranches to the north.

# 28

The Chiricahua left their camp behind the Running Bird's barn several hours before sunrise. They climbed the hill behind the barn, Mangus leading the way. They climbed quickly, passing silently among the trees. Thousands of stars provided weak but ample light for them.

Mangus was followed by Gil-lee, Taza, and Loco. Gil-lee carried the beef jerky that was their lunch and a cowhide, Taza and Loco each carried a cowhide. Mahko had gone first, some 30 minutes ahead, to scout trail. He was leaving sign marking the trail they were to follow, sign that only a Chiricahua would recognize in the dark.

They reached the crest of the hill, stopped a moment, and started down into the valley, still following Makho's trail. When they reached the valley floor, Makho was waiting for them crouched behind a large rock. Using sign language, Makho described the path they would take to reach the stand of cottonwoods by the river then abruptly stood and moved off at a slow jog, staying as low to the ground as possible. The others followed after him without hesitation.

They reached the stand of cottonwoods about an hour before sunrise. They chose a hollow in the middle of the stand that afforded almost perfect cover and settled to the ground to wait for daylight. Loco volunteered to stay awake and stand guard so the others could sleep. The other four accepted without comment, lay down, and were soon asleep.

As the sky to the east began to lighten, Loco awakened the others. They came awake immediately, quietly, ready. They each ate a small ration of beef jerky and drank water from the river then turned to Makho.

Makho said, "Today we scout the large herd on the mornin' side of the river. Tomorrow we scout the large herd on the afternoon side of the river. On the following four days we scout many of the smaller bunches on both sides of the river."

Makho looked at each of the other Chiricahua. No response was forthcoming, so he continued, "To scout the herds, three of us will go among them under cowhides for two hours and return. Then the two who stayed will go under cowhides for two hours and return. The first man-cows will be Gil-lee, Taza, and Loco. The second man-cows will be Mangus and me. Those of us who remain here will use the spyglass and watch for anyone comin' in our direction."

Makho looked again at each of the others. No response was forthcoming, so he continued, "When the second man-cows return, we will hide the cowhides here in the cottonwoods and return to the Runnin' Bird to report what we found."

Makho looked at each of the others for a third time. No response was forthcoming, so he continued, "Gil-lee, Taza, Loco, go now."

Gil-lee, Taza, and Loco each picked up a cowhide and walked to the edge of the stand of cottonwoods. They put the cowhides over their shoulders and tied the rawhide thongs attached to the hides where the cows necks had been around their own necks. There were rawhide thongs on the inside of the front and hind legs of the cowhides that they tied around their own arms and legs. Standing, they appeared strange, but as they left the trees walking bent over at the waist, they appeared much more like the cattle they were imitating.

The three man-cows entered the herd separately, slowly moving among the cattle looking at brands. The cattle didn't seem to be bothered by the man-cows moving slowly among them. All the cattle they saw had Bar CS brands and were branded on the right flank. When two-hours had passed, they returned to the cottonwoods, removed their cowhides, and were glad to be able to stand upright again.

Mangus and Makho took two of the cowhides, went to the edge of the stand of cottonwoods, put the cowhides over their shoulders, and fastened them around their necks, arms, and legs. They bent over at the waist and slowly entered the herd as the previous man-cows had done before them. They found the same, all the cattle had Bar CS brands and were branded on the right flank. When their two-hours had passed, they returned to the cottonwoods.

Makho said, "Taza and Loco, clear a site large enough to hide the cowhides and bury them under branches and leaves. Then, let's eat and rest. When the sun is well past noon, we'll leave for the Runnin' Bird and tell what we found. We'll return using a different trail than we took to get here. Be extremely careful, its daylight and we could be easily seen leavin' the valley. Stay in low places and behind brush. Do not stand or walk upright. I'll leave first, select the trail, and make sure it's safe. Follow my trail as you did this mornin', Mangus will again lead you."

Makho looked at each of the others. No response was forthcoming, so he took his share of the last of the jerky and found a shady place to rest until it was time to leave. The other four followed his lead and took their shares of the remaining jerky and rested.

When he felt it was time, Makho rose and left, crossing the river noiselessly. He stayed low and behind the scrub, jogging across the valley floor and up the hill. Every so often he knelt down and marked his trail.

Some fifteen minutes later the others followed Makho in the same sequence they had come, Mangus, Gil-lee, Taza, and Loco. They followed the trail markers left by Makho, seeing Bar CS hands, but not being seen by them. They arrived at the top of the hill and met Makho, who was sitting on the boulder pile waiting for them. They found places to sit and rested.

Mangus said, "My brothers, we have been successful today. We have gone peacefully into the valley of the enemy and returned unharmed. We have done well. May we be as successful tomorrow."

He looked at each of the others. Each responded by nodding his head. He said, "It is time to go," as he rose and started down the hill. When they arrived at their camp, Gil-lee, Taza, and Loco began preparing their evening meal, and Mangus and Makho went to report to Bird.

# 29

I woke early again inside a very dark, almost black bunkhouse. The only light there was came from the twinkling of the thousands of stars outside glowing in through the open bunkhouse window. I didn't hear another person. Ranch hands at the Running Bird rose and started early, earlier than I, it seemed.

I was certain I was the last person on the Running Bird to awaken, again. I was also certain the Chiricahua had awakened earlier than I and were well on their way to the Bar CS.

I rolled out from my bedroll under the blanket John Fields had left for me and put on my pants, socks, boots, and gun belt. I went outside, poured water into the tin bowl, washed, and combed my hair with wet fingers. I dried with the towel I found hanging from a nail and put on my shirt. I noticed it was a clean, dry towel this morning.

It was just beginning to lighten at the horizon in the east. I had awakened at almost the same time I had the day before. And, I was certain the morning activities I witnessed the day before would be happening again today. The daily ranch routine on the Running Bird probably didn't vary much from day-to-day.

I picked up my eight-gauge, walked to the bunkhouse porch, and found a place at the table at the end of one of the benches. I was ready for breakfast. I had a lot of riding to do today and would need the energy, so I filled my plate with eggs, meat, and potatoes, and took a slab of bread and some butter. John Fields brought me a cup of coffee.

I nodded at him in appreciation.

When the pace of eating slowed, John Fields stood up and gave the day's assignments as he had the day before. The assignments again seemed fair, not a single hand complained about his or asked for a change. One by one the hands excused themselves from the table taking their plates, cups, and flatware and placing them in the appropriate bucket of warm water to the side of the kitchen door. From there they scattered, to begin their assigned tasks.

My plan for today and tomorrow was to ride to the four ranches to the north of the Running Bird and inquire about any trouble they'd had with the Bar CS and if they'd recently lost any cattle. I had a fair distance to ride not only to the first ranch, but between the four ranches. I had to leave soon and I had to pack a kit to take with me, since I wouldn't return until tomorrow sometime, and I'd probably have to sleep out on the trail tonight.

I went back into the bunkhouse, packed my bedroll and kit, and carried it back with me to the table on the porch. I dropped both the bedroll and the kit on the floor and went to the bunkhouse kitchen for another cup of coffee. I had time to drink it while my horse finished breakfast. Then I would tack up and leave for my visits to the Open A, Long X, Running W, and Bar M. Though these ranches shared common borders, their ranch houses were a fair piece from each other.

It was about seven o'clock when I led my horse out of the barn, brushed him, checked and cleaned his feet, and tacked him up with saddle pads, saddle and cinch, breast collar, and bridle with bit and reins. I tied my halter with a lead rope attached to the saddle's front right leather strings. A change of clothes and food for three meals on the trail were in my saddle bags. I threw the saddle bags over the saddle skirt behind the cantle and tied them in place. I put my bedroll and slicker wrapped coat over the saddle bags behind the cantle and tied them on securely. I put my Winchester in its scabbard tied to the left side at the front of the saddle, running down from above the pommel almost to the stirrup.

I mounted, holding the reins and some mane in my left hand and my eight-gauge in my right. I took a last look at the tranquility of the ranch and pressed my calves against my horse's lower sides, pushing him into a jog trot through the main gate and out onto the trail leading north. Once we were comfortably moving along, I placed my eight-gauge across the pommel of my saddle, in front of the horn with the leather thong attached to the ring on the breach looped over the horn. It would mostly balance there at a walk or a jog trot, though I'd have to adjust its position every so often. I'd certainly have to hold on to it at an extended trot, lope, or faster gait.

We alternated between a flat walk, jog trot, and lope. Whenever we crossed a stream, I stopped to let him blow and drink and have a mouthful or two of grass. After about two hours, I stopped under a large spreading pine and dismounted. He really appreciated getting rid of me. He shook starting from his head through to his tail, stretched, and got the kinks out. When he was finished, he looked happy and satisfied. Fifteen minutes rest and I remounted and we continued on, alternating between a flat walk, jog trot, and lope. We stopped at streams to let him blow and drink.

About an hour and a half later we arrived at the Open A. As I rode up to the barn and dismounted, Jim Slatter, the foreman, came out of the barn to meet me.

Jim said, "Mornin', Emmett. I'm really glad you're here. I need to talk with you 'bout what's happenin' here 'bouts."

"Good mornin', Jim," I replied. "I'm glad to be here. I probably want to talk with you 'bout the same thin' you want to talk with me, rustlin'."

"Yes, you're right. Come into the house and let's talk over a cup of coffee. Hungry?"

"Jim, that's a welcome invitation. First, I need to take care of my horse, give him from fresh water, tie him to the hitchin' rack, and loosen his cinch."

"Of course. I'll have one of my hands take care of him for you."

Jim called one of his hands over. He took my horse and started walking him toward the watering trough.

I said, "Thank you. I'm really dry and hungry and definitely in need of a cup of coffee, though I could really use some water first."

We stopped at a small water pump at the corner of the barn and I filled and drank a couple of dippers of water. We continued on to the house, climbed up the three stairs to the porch, went in the house through the front door, and settled in the dining room. Jim went into the kitchen and asked the cook to serve us lunch in the house before he served lunch to the hands outside by the barn. Jim returned to the dining room with two mugs of coffee.

Jim said, "Emmett, please tell me what's on your mind."

I replied, "Jim, we heard that the ranches in this area have been losin' cattle since the Bar CS moved into the valley to the east."

"I've been losin' cattle, a few head at a time, between ten and 20 a week. They just seem to disappear. We know where they were grazing, but when we look for 'em later, they're gone. I guess I've lost 100 head so far. And, I hear that I'm not alone. Other ranchers are experiencin' the same, some've lost more."

"Have you put out guards at night?"

"I've thought about that, but my hands aren't gunman. I don't want to start the shootin'. We'd probably be outgunned and I don't want any of my hands hurt. I've been waitin' for the opportunity to talk with you or Alexander. What are you plannin' to do?"

"Right now I'm gatherin' information. I'm visitin' the ten ranches in the area, four today, three the day after tomorrow, and the last three two days after that, to learn what's been happenin'. We'll put together a plan after that."

"That's what I wanted to hear, thank you. Do you want my help?"

"No! You're right. You and your hands aren't gunman. We don't want any of you hurt. If we're successful in getting' your cattle back, you'll have to come get 'em."

Jim nodded.

Just then, the cook came into the dining room with lunch. We stopped our conversation and filled our plates. After we finished lunch and had another cup of coffee, I went out, collected my horse, tightened my cinch, checked the rest of my tack and kit, and left for the Long X.

We walked out to the road and turned north. After about five minutes, I pressed my calves against the horse's lower sides, pushing him into a jog trot. We alternated between a flat walk, jog trot, and lope for about an hour and reached the Long X. When we came to the ranch house, Jay Rolf, the ranch foreman, met me.

We exchanged pleasantries and discussed their cattle situation. Their experience was similar to that of the Open A, though they had lost more cattle, about 150 head. I explained about my fact finding trip and asked Jay not to do anything to jeopardize any potential plan we would develop. He agreed and I left for the Running W and the Bar M, where I had similar discussions.

The sun was getting low toward the western horizon as I was leaving the Bar M. I decided to double back on my trail heading for the Open A to spend the night, maybe even get dinner and breakfast, too. I'd have to leave early in the morning to get back to the Running Bird in the afternoon to meet with Bird.

# 30

The Chiricahua left for the Bar CS on the second morning several hours before sunrise. They made it to the stand of cottonwoods next to the river undetected about an hour before and rested until sunup. Just after the sun came over the hills to the east, Gil-lee, Taza, and Loco tied on cowhides and went out among the large herd on the afternoon side of the stream. The cattle didn't seem to notice, or at least, didn't pay any attention to them. After two hours, Gil-lee, Taza, and Loco returned and Mangus and Makho put on the cowhides and went out among the cattle. After their two hours, Mangus and Makho returned.

Makho looked at the others and said, "I only saw Bar CS brands on the cattle. Did you see any other?"

Each of the others shook his head indicating no.

Makho continued, "Taza and Loco, bury the cowhides under branches and leaves as you did yesterday. Bury them so we can easily find them and use them tomorrow, then let's eat and rest. In about an hour we'll leave for the Runnin' Bird and tell what we've found. We'll return usin' a different path than we used to get here. We must be extremely careful, since the sun is high and we could be easily noticed. Stay in low places and behind brush. Don't stand or walk upright. I'll leave first and select the trail, making sure it's safe. Follow my trail. Mangus will lead you back."

Makho looked at each of the others. They gave no response, so he took his share of the last of the jerky and found a shady place to rest until it was time to leave. The other four followed his lead, taking their shares of the remaining jerky and resting.

When he felt it was time to leave, Makho rose and left, crossing the river noiselessly. He stayed low, behind the scrub, jogging across the valley floor and up the hill. Every so often he knelt down and marked the trail for those who would follow.

Some fifteen minutes after Makho left, the other four followed in the same sequence in which they had came, Mangus, Gil-lee, Taza, and last, Loco. They followed the trail markers left by Makho, seeing riders in the distance, but not being seen by them. After about an hour and a half, they arrived at the top of the hill and met Makho, who was sitting on the pile of boulders waiting for them as he had yesterday. They sat near him and rested.

Mangus said, "My brothers, we have had another successful day. We have gone peacefully into the valley of the enemy and returned unharmed. We have done well. May we be as successful tomorrow."

He looked at each of the others. Each responded by nodding his head. Mangus said, "It is time to return to the Runnin' Bird," as he rose and started down the hill.

When they arrived at their camp, Bird was waiting for them. Gil-lee, Taza, and Loco began preparing their evening meal while Mangus and Makho sat with Bird.

Bird said, "My brothers, how was your day?"

Makho answered, "Bird, our man-cows passed among the large herd on the afternoon side of the stream. As yesterday, we saw only the Bar CS brand on the cattle."

"Are you sure?"

"Yes.  You told us they originally brought some 2,000 head into the valley.  That would be the approximate number of cattle in the two large herds together.  It may be that the smaller bunches were taken from the ranches and stay together, not joinin' the larger herds."

"Yes, that could be.  You'll begin scoutin' the smaller bunches tomorrow?"

"Yes, that is our plan.  Over the next four days we will scout the smaller bunches and their two camps, the main camp next to the river and the smaller camps on the north side of the valley."

"Thank you.  That is a big help.  May you have continued success.  I return to my house.  Eat and rest until you leave for the Bar CS again in the mornin'."

Makho and Mangus nodded at Bird, who rose and left them. Bird walked to the bunkhouse kitchen for a cup of coffee, which he took to a table on the porch at the side of the bunkhouse.

I returned to the Running Bird mid-afternoon from visiting the four ranches to the north.  I dismounted in front of the barn and leaned my eight-gauge against the hitching rail.  I changed my bridle for a halter and tied my horse to the hitching rail. Next, I took my Winchester out of its scabbard and leaned it against the hitching rail next to my eight-gauge.  Then I took my slicker wrapped coat, bedroll, saddlebags, breast collar, saddle, and saddle pads off of my horse and carried them and my bridle into the barn and put them all on a saddle rack hanging from the barn wall.  I untied my horse and turned him loose in a small paddock to stretch, roll, and drink.  I would come back later to brush him and put him in a stall with his dinner.

I went to the bunkhouse to wash and brush my clothes clean as best I could. I noticed I was really hungry. I had been riding the better part of six hours without stopping to eat. So, I went to the bunkhouse kitchen to get a late lunch. When I came out of the bunkhouse kitchen with a cup of coffee and a plate of food, I found Bird sitting at one of the tables at the side of the bunkhouse with a cup of coffee.

I sat across the table from him and between bites said, "It's good to be back. I rode a fair piece and learned a lot. I'm really tired. After lunch, I'll have to sleep. So, while I'm eating, let's discuss what the Chiricahua and I discovered yesterday and today."

"If it's alright with you, I'll tell you about the Chiricahua first so you can eat."

"Good idea."

Bird continued, "Both yesterday and today they left here for the Bar CS well before sunrise and arrived there with 'bout an hour of darkness left. They hid in the stand of cottonwoods next to the river in the middle of the valley. They took three cowhides with 'em and after sunrise took two-hour turns wearin' the cowhides movin' among the two larger herds lookin' at brands. They call themselves man-cows when they're wearin' the cowhides. The only brand they saw both days was the Bar CS. Both days they returned here by mid-afternoon. Tomorrow and the day after, they'll move among the smaller bunches of cattle looking at brands. The two days after that they will scout the Bar CS main camp and the three smaller ranches at the north side of the valley."

I thought for a while and said, "They should find stolen cattle in the smaller bunches. It makes sense that the stolen cattle would stay to themselves unless forced to merge with one of the main herds."

"Yes, that's possible."

"Is there more?"

"No."

So I began recounting my trip, "Day before yesterday I visited the Open A, the Long X, the Running W, and the Bar M. The foremen were very happy to see me. Each told basically the same story. They began noticin' small bunches of cattle missin', maybe ten to 20 at a time, but not from their main herds. The cattle went missin' from outlyin' areas of their ranches. And it started for all of them at about the same time, a couple of weeks ago. Each of them has been hit three or four times, meanin' they've each lost between 40 and 60 head for a total of between 150 and 240 head. If the other five ranches have been hit the same, the combined total could be double that. And, adding in your losses, we're lookin' at over 500 head missing. These are not isolated incidents. This is organized rustlin', a major problem."

Bird nodded.

"Please draw the brands of all ten ranches, those of the Runnin' Bird and the other nine, for the Chiricahua. With the pictures, they'll be able to tell us which they've seen."

Bird again nodded.

"Good. I'm all in. I'm gonna go take care of my horse and sleep. I'll get up early tomorrow morning and leave for the three ranches to the west."

I rose from the table, smiled and nodded at Bird, took my plate and utensils, and dropped them into the proper buckets next to the bunkhouse kitchen door. I doggedly went to the paddock, gathered up my horse, gave him a good grooming, and put him in a stall in the barn with a full bucket of water and his dinner, an large armful of hay.

I was overly tired and went straight to the bunkhouse, spread out my bedroll, and lay down on my bunk. I was snug inside my bedroll, and the blanket helped. I was asleep as soon as I closed my eyes.

The next four days repeated the preceding two. On the first day, I rode to the three ranches to the west of the Running Bird, the Circle R, the Hashknife, and the Rafter J and returned to the Running Bird the next day. On the third day, I rode to the two ranches, south of the Running Bird, the Flying O and the N Bar N and returned to the Running Bird the following day. On the days I returned, Bird and I met and discussed my trips and what the Chiricahua had seen on their visits to the Bar CS.

I learned from my visits to the five ranches to the south and west similar information to what I learned on visit to the four ranches to the north, cattle were missing. Small bunches of them going missing one or more times a week. Bird told me the Chiricahua had examined many of the small bunches of cattle. A few of the cattle in the small bunches carried Bar CS brands, but most had brands from the other ranches, either run with Bar CS or still carrying their original brands.

Now we had confirmed where the missing were and who had taken them.

# 31

For the fourth morning in the last seven I woke inside a very dark, almost black bunkhouse. As on the other three mornings, the only light was the twinkling of thousands of stars glowing in through the open window. I didn't hear anyone else in the bunkhouse. I was certain I was the last person on the Running Bird to awaken, again.

I rolled out from out of my bedroll and the blanket John Fields had given me and put on pants, socks, boots, and gun belt. I picked up my eight-gauge and my shirt and went outside. I leaned the eight-gauge against the side of the bunkhouse and hung my shirt on the nail. I poured water from the water pitcher into the tin bowl and washed and combed my hair with wet fingers. I dried with another clean towel hanging from the nail and put on my shirt. I noticed it was beginning to lighten at the horizon in the east and wondered how a clean towel magically appeared every morning and the water pitcher became full here at the back of the bunkhouse.

I picked up my eight-gauge, walked around to the bunkhouse porch, and found a place at the table at the end of one of the benches where I sat. I put the butt of my eight-gauge on the floor and leaned its barrel against the edge of the table. I filled my plate with eggs, meat, and potatoes, and took a slab of bread and some butter from the platters being passed around the table. John Fields brought me a cup of coffee.

I said to him, "Much 'preciated. Thank you."

When the pace of eating slowed, John Fields stood up and gave the day's assignments. The assignments again seemed fair, not a single hand complained about his or asked for a change. One by one the hands excused themselves from the table taking their plates, cups, and flatware and placing them in the appropriate bucket of warm water to the side of the kitchen door. From there they scattered, to begin their assigned tasks.

After I finished my breakfast and put my plate, cup, and flatware in the wash buckets, I went back into the bunkhouse, rolled up my bedroll, packed my kit, and returned to the table on the porch. I dropped my bedroll and kit near my eight-gauge and went to the bunkhouse kitchen for another cup of coffee. I had time to drink it while my horse finished breakfast. Then I would tack up and leave for Sunrise.

It was about seven o'clock when I led my horse out of the barn, curried him, checked and cleaned his feet, and tacked him up with saddle pads, saddle and girth, breast collar, and bridle with bit and reins, then tied my halter with a lead rope attached to the saddle's front right leather strings. My dirty clothes were in my saddle bags. I threw the saddle bags over the saddle skirt behind the cantle and tied them in place with the saddle's rear leather strings. I put my bedroll over the saddle bags and then the slicker wrapped coat and tied all of them on together with the rear saddle strings. I finished by putting my Winchester in its scabbard tied to the left side of the front of the saddle, running down from above the pommel almost to the stirrup.

I mounted holding the reins and some mane in my left hand and my eight-gauge in my right. I took a last look at the tranquility of the ranch and pressed my calves against my horse's lower sides, pushing him into a jog trot out through the main gate and onto the trail toward Sunrise. Once we were comfortably moving along, I placed my eight-gauge across the pommel of my saddle, in front of the horn with the leather thong attached to the ring on the breach looped over the horn.

We alternated between a flat walk, a jog trot, and a lope. Every half hour I stopped to let him blow and have a couple mouthfuls of grass. After about two hours and again after another two hours, I pulled up and dismounted in the shade of a tree. Fifteen minutes rest and I remounted and we continued on, stopping at streams to blow and drink. Just after noon we entered Sunrise and went straight to the livery where I dismounted, unsaddled my horse, brushed him down, and turned him loose in the large paddock next to the barn. The hands at the livery would see to it that he had water and was put into a stall and fed after he cooled down.

I walked from the livery to the marshal's office in City Hall. Alexander and Lacy were waiting for me. Alexander looked annoyed, he said, "We've been waitin' for you so long we're both 'bout dead from starvation. Don't sit down, it's time for lunch. Just put your stuff down, turn around, and head out the door for the Chicago House. We'll be right behind you pushin' you along to go faster."

We ordered lunch, steak, potato, rolls, butter, and coffee, and I began telling them what Bird, the Chiricahua, and I did and learned over the previous six days. By the time I finished, our lunch had come and we had cleaned our plates. Alexander and Lacy sat quietly as my story sank in.

Alexander asked, "You visited all nine of the ranches to the north, west, and south and Bird told you 'bout what's been happenin' at the Running Bird. The Chiricahua scouted the Bar CS herd and found proof of rustlin', a large number of cattle with other ranch's brands in the Bar CS herd. And, the Chiricahua verified what you already knew about their headquarters and the small ranches at the north side of the valley."

I answered, "Yes, sounds 'bout right. What they found new 'bout the small ranches is there are three men at the middle ranch. No-one at the other two. And, they don't seem to have any weapons, or at least don't carry any."

"All the ranches, the Bar CS, the Runnin' Bird, and the other nine, are not within our jurisdiction. We have no authority out there. Before we can go there and do anythin', Knight'll have to deputize us."

Lacy and I nodded in agreement.

"We have to create a basic plan this afternoon for takin' down the Bar CS that we can present to everyone tomorrow. I'm sure they won't accept our plan right off and will want changes, but they'll expect us to have one."

Lacy and I nodded in agreement and I replied, "If it's alright with you, I'll lay out a plan and you can add to it or change it when I'm finished."

"Go right ahead," encouraged Alexander.

"We ride out as a group to the Runnin' Bird after midnight tomorrow night. We should get there before sunrise so if Bar CS hands are watching the Runnin' Bird they won't see us come in."

I stopped and waited for Alexander to comment. He said, "Alright so far, keep goin'."

"We hide our horses in the barn and go to the bunkhouse porch for breakfast. After breakfast we sleep in the bunkhouse, since we all should be tired after our night ride."

I stopped again and waited for Alexander. He said, "OK."

"We should be awake by noon. Bird and the Chiricahua take us up the hill behind the barn and show us the Bar CS and point out things we'll need to know."

"Keep goin'."

"We go back down the hill to the bunkhouse for lunch and refine our plan."

Alexander thought for a while and said, "Well, Emmett, that's good, far as it goes, but it's only a start. I thought you went to West Point. There's nothin' in your plan about how we're goin' to get there undetected, how we're goin' to confront them without a bitter gunfight, and most importantly, how we're goin' to capture Stockett, Vargas, and the Bar CS hands. Knight will want them to stand trial for rustlin'. And, we have to save the whole herd, since we need to return the rustled cattle to their owners and we'll need to put the Bar CS cattle in protective custody. But, I don't know what we're goin' to do with the Bar CS cattle unless you and I are goin' to start running the Bar CS ourselves."

"Alexander, you're right, as usual. My plan is incomplete."

"Well, finish it. Now!"

"The Chiricahua left the Runnin' Bird for the Bar CS on foot several hours before sunrise on six successive days, startin' seven days ago, and we know they arrived at the stand of cottonwoods in the middle of the Bar CS just before sunrise. We'll want to arrive at the Bar CS main tent camp, which is near the stand of cottonwoods and where the majority of the hands will be just before sunrise. To do that, we'll have to leave at about the same time the Chiricahua did. However, we won't be able to go on foot, our boots are no good for walking that far. We'll have to ride, but our horses and tack make too much noise. We'll leave everythin' non-essential at the Runnin' Bird and wrap our horses' feet and snouts with rags. We'll split up at the edge of the meadow, Bird and the Chiricahua will go take out the night crew and keep the herd intact. Knight and Every will go out to the three small spreads near the north hills to round up the hands stationed there, and the rest of us will go to their main camp and surprise and capture Stockett, Vargas, and the Bar CS hands not out with the herd."

"Much better, Emmett. Lacy, what do you think?"

Lacy answered, "I like it."

Alexander finished the discussion with, "As with any plan, it's good until the ball goes up, then everythin'll change."

# 32

Bird woke before sunrise, dressed, ate, and walked to the Chiricahua camp behind the barn. They were awake, sitting around a small fire waiting for him. They offered coffee and jerky, which Bird accepted graciously. They talked a while about their trip to Sunrise and what they were to accomplish. Then, together, they went to the corral next to the barn, caught up their horses, tied them to the corral fence, curried them, and made ready to leave. They mounted and rode out the front gate toward Sunrise at a jog trot.

== < > ==

Knight and Every woke early and met at Sweet's Café for breakfast. They were to take the early afternoon train to Sunrise. After breakfast they returned to their rooms to pack, bedrolls, clothes, guns, and ammunition. They met again at the Sheriffs Office where they passed a quiet morning. At about noon, they left the office in the hands of another deputy and went to lunch at Sweet's Café. After lunch they went to the livery, collected and curried their horses, tacked up, loaded their bedrolls and kits on their saddles and walked leading their horses to the train station. Knight purchased their tickets and passage for their horses to Sunrise. When the train arrived, they loaded their horses into the stock car and boarded the rear passenger car, which was directly in front of the stock car.

== < > ==

Dyson and Jackson spent the morning at the trial of a man suspected of robbing the Penance Mercantile and killing its proprietor. Although the court said he was a suspect until convicted, he had been caught in the act by Dyson and Jackson and everyone knew he was guilty before the trial started. The trial was just a formality and was over almost as soon as it started with a guilty verdict. The guilty man was immediately taken out to a large tree behind the livery and hung.

After the hanging, Dyson and Jackson had lunch at the saloon and returned to their rooms to pack, bedrolls, clothes, guns, and ammunition. They met at the livery to collect and ready their horses and load their bedrolls and its on their saddles. They walked, leading their horses, to the train station and purchased their tickets and passage for their horses to Sunrise. When the train arrived, they loaded their horses into the stock car and boarded the rear passenger car. They noticed Knight and Every in the car and took the empty seat facing them.

== < > ==

The train arrived in Sunrise late in the afternoon. Knight, Every, Dyson, and Jackson climbed down from the rear passenger car, went to the stock car, unloaded their horses, and walked them to the livery. They took their bedrolls and kits off their saddles, stripped the tack from their horses, and turned them loose in the corral next to the barn. The livery hands would round them up, put them in stalls, curry them, and feed and water them just before dark.

After leaving their horses at the livery, Knight, Every, Dyson, and Jackson walked to City Hall to the marshal's office where Bird, the five Chiricahua, Alexander, Lacy, and I were waiting for them.

Bird was the first to speak, "How was the iron horse?"

Knight replied, "My saddle's more comfortable, but the train got here faster than my horse would've. The train don't stop to eat every durn clump of green grass it passes."

Bird laughed, "You should ride with the Chiricahua. You wouldn't slow down, stop, or rest. You'd get where you were goin' faster'n you'd ever thought possible. And, you wouldn't have a saddle to relax in."

Dyson responded with a smile, "Without a saddle, it'd hurt too much to ride. It'd be torture."

Alexander said, "I'm hungry and I bet you all are, too. Let's go over to the Chicago House for dinner. I've arranged with Ward Layne to close the restaurant and prepare dinner just for us. It should be ready now."

Everyone voiced agreement and we left for the Chicago House. As Alexander said, the restaurant was closed and reserved for us. The tables had been arranged for us to sit together. Alexander at the head with Lacy and me to his left and right. Knight, Every, Dyson, and Jackson at the other end, and Bird and the five Chiricahua three to a side in between.

As soon as we were seated, drinks were served, water for the Chiricahua, water and whiskey for us, and coffee for any who wanted it. Then came dinner, steak, potatoes, beans, and bread and butter. There was little talking while we ate, we were too hungry and the food was too good.

When we had eaten our fill, Alexander said, "A lot has happened since Lacy went to visit Knight and Every in Trinidad, and Dyson and Jackson in Penance. Because you need to know the latest before we make plans, Emmett and Bird will tell you what they've done and what they've learned. Emmett, whyn't you start?"

I stood, acknowledged each one at the table individually by name or a nod and began, "As you know, Bird came to us and told us he was losin' cattle, a few head at a time, and his losses were growin'. We were certain that if Bird was losin' cattle, the ranches close to him would be, too. So, I rode to the Runnin' Bird, looked over the Bar CS valley, and saw a very large herd. I spent the next six days visitin' the nine ranches to the north, west, and south of the Runnin' Bird. I didn't go to the ranches to the east, because I'd have had to ride all the way around the Bar CS to get to 'em. It would've taken too long. I asked at the nine ranches about cattle losses. They had all lost cattle in similar numbers as Bird. It seemed the total loss was at least, but probably more than 500 head."

No-one said anything.

Alexander turned to Bird and said, "Bird, your turn."

Bird stood, and as I had, acknowledged each one at the table individually by name or a nod and started, "After I visited Alexander, Emmett, and Lacy and told them what was happenin' at the Runnin' Bird, I rode to the Chiricahua res to get help. Five Chiricahua agreed to come here with me. They are here with us: Gil-lee, Loco, Mahko, Mangus, and Taza. These are not their names but names of chiefs from long ago. Names they've chosen to be called while they're here with us. They're stayin' with me at the Runnin' Bird. They went into the Bar CS valley for six straight days. The first four days they looked at brands on cattle. To not scare the cattle and not be seen by Bar CS hands, they went into the herd two or three at a time wearin' cowhides. The

179

cattle in the two large herds all had the Bar CS brand. Cattle in smaller bunches had brands from ten other ranches."

Bird stopped and waited for a response, there was none, so he continued.

"The last two days they spent at the three small ranches at the north side of the valley. There are three men there. It appears they do not carry weapons. They seems to be farmin' and carin' for equipment. It doesn't appear they're involved in the rustlin'."

From a sitting position, Alexander said, "As you heard, we know ten ranches have recently lost cattle and their cattle have been found at the Bar CS. There are only two ways those cattle could have come to be at the Bar CS, they could've been purchased by the Bar CS, or the Bar CS stole 'em. Since we know the Bar CS didn't purchase 'em, they had to've stole 'em. That's rustlin'. It's time to get the cattle back and to deal with the Bar CS, its owner, Charles Stockett, and its foreman, Ed Vargas. Are you in with us?"

Knight, Every, Dyson, and Jackson enthusiastically said they were. Bird and the Chiricahua sat quietly.

Alexander continued, "First, Emmett, Lacy, and I and Dyson, Jackson, Bird and the Chiricahua have no jurisdiction in the area where the Runnin' Bird and the Bar CS are located. Rawlins, you'll have to deputize everyone at the table so we can act with authority."

Knight responded, "Of course. I've never deputized an Indian, but there's always a first time. Consider yourselves deputized."

Alexander said, "Second, Emmett, Lacy, and I created a plan last night which Emmett will present to you. We'll discuss the plan and finalize it. We all have to agree to the plan and it has to be sufficiently detailed that each of us knows where he's to be and what he's to do. There are too many of 'em and too few of us for us to be ill prepared. But first, let's take a break. I need to relieve myself and I want more coffee, whiskey, and dessert."

We stood. Several went outside to find a tree or use the outhouse. Alexander called to Clay to bring another bottle of whiskey, a fresh pot of coffee, and a couple of pies. When everyone returned, we began in earnest.

I stood, moved behind my chair, and pushed it up to the table. I presented to the group the plan Alexander, Lacy, and I created the night before, "The Chiricahua left the Runnin' Bird for the Bar CS on foot several hours before sunrise. They arrived at the stand of cottonwoods in the middle of the Bar CS just before sunrise. Since we want to arrive at the Bar CS main camp, which is near the stand of cottonwoods and where the majority of Bar CS hands will be just before sunrise, we'll have to leave at about the same time they did. However, we won't be able to go on foot, our boots are no good for walking that far. We'll have to ride, but our horses and tack make too much noise. We'll wrap our horses' feet and snouts with rags. When we get to the edge of the tree line in the valley, we'll split up. Bird and the Chiricahua will head into the herd and take out the night crew and keep the herd intact. The rest of us, except Knight and Every, will go to the main camp and capture Stockett, Vargas, and the rest of the Bar CS hands. Knight and Every will ride around to the north side of the valley and capture the hands at the ranches there."

Alexander waited for me to sit, then said, "Bird and the Chiricahua will decide how they'll do their part once they enter the herd. Knight and Every will figure out how they'll do their part once they arrive at the three small ranches. For the rest of us, I'd like to hear your ideas."

Knight took the lead and answered, "Alexander, we expect you to lead this action and tell us what to do."

Everyone began speaking at once, agreeing with Knight.

Alexander interrupted them saying as he rose from the table, "Alright. Let's split into three groups. Bird and the Chiricahua, Knight and Every, and the rest of us. Think 'bout your part and decide how you'll do it. Now, go get some rest. We'll meet at the livery at midnight and leave for the Runnin' Bird. We'll finalize the plan tomorrow after we take a look at the Bar CS from up on the hill. Good night."

Bird and the Chiricahua walked out the back of the Chicago House, collected their horses, and left for the Running Bird at an extended trot. Knight and Every went through the front batwing doors on their way to the livery to discuss their part and get some rest. Alexander, Lacy, Dyson, Jackson and I sat around the table discussing our part for another hour or so.

Finally, Alexander got up and left out the front batwing doors on his way home. Lacy and I climbed the stairs to our individual rooms in the Chicago House. I unlocked the door to my room, stepped inside, and relocked the door, as Jewel Scarlet's melodic voice came from the bed, "Emmett, you sure keep a woman waiting."

# 33

We met at the livery at midnight. I was the last to arrive, I had been detained by Jewel Marion, who wouldn't let me leave without, as she called it, properly saying goodbye to me.

We wore coats and carried our Winchesters, bedrolls, slickers, and saddle bags packed with clothes, extra and Colts and ammunition. I was also carrying my eight-gauge. There was a buckboard at the side of the barn, we deposited our stuff in it as we arrived. We came close to filling its bed.

Lacy pointed at the buckboard and said, "Probably best if we brought the buckboard. It'd make it easier on us and our horses."

I said, "Good idea."

Alexander said, "Yes, good idea. Emmett, you'll drive the buckboard. Have one of the livery hands get a good pulling horse and hitch it up."

I said, "Yes, Alexander," and went off to find someone.

We collected our horses from their stalls and brought them outside to the hitching rail. We curried them, checked and cleaned their feet, and tacked up. By the time we were ready, a livery hand had a horse hitched to the buckboard and had run a rope crosswise over our stuff to make sure none of it would be lost along the way. I tied my bridle onto the saddle with the front leather strings, leaving the halter and lead rope on my horse. I gave the end of the lead rope to Lacy, climbed up onto the buckboard's bench, and laid my eight-gauge on the bench beside me.

Alexander looked us over and said, "Lacy, you're at the rear as drag behind Emmett in the buckboard." He hesitated then said to me, "Emmett, what do you say to get a troop started?"

"Move out," I replied. "Though, you gotta say it loud enough to have it understood as a command."

Alexander smiled and shouted, "MOVE OUT."

And we did. Alexander in the lead, followed by Knight and Every riding abreast, Dyson and Jackson riding abreast, me in the buckboard, and Lacy, the drag.

There was no moon, it was nearly dark. The only light came from thousands of stars spread across the sky. We headed north out of Sunrise toward Penance at a walk until we were out of town, then pushed our horses into a jog trot to eat up the distance. After a while we came to the fork, straight ahead was Penance and to the right was the Running Bird, the Bar CS, and eventually Kansas.

We stopped at the fork to let the horses blow, stomp and snort, starting out again at a jog trot, taking the right track. We stopped every so often to rest the horses and at the streams to let them drink.

When I had returned alone on this same route from the Running Bird two days ago, it had taken me under five hours. Because there were seven of us and the buckboard, we were going much slower than I had. It took us just over six hours to reach the small valley just to the west of the Running Bird, the one frequented by the gray leopard appaloosa stallion and his mares. As we crossed his valley, the stallion trumpeted at us declaring we were in his territory. We could see his mares lying on the ground behind him. We rode eastward through the middle of the valley until we crested the hill overlooking the Running Bird. We stopped on the crest and took in the view. The sun was just coming over the hills to the east, a spectacular, cool, crisp sunrise.

We walked our horses down the hill, stopping in front of the barn. Everyone except me dismounted from his horse, and stood next to it, giving the horses a minute to cool down before being put up. I drove the buckboard alongside the barn, climbed down from the seat, and unhitched the horse. We walked all the horses into the barn and tied them to tie rings attached to the stalls. We stripped our tack and put all of it on saddle trees attached to the wall of the barn. We rubbed the horses down, put them in individual stalls, and gave them water and hay to keep them busy.

John Fields met us as we exited the barn. He said, "Our hands are out roundin' up our herd. They won't be back for a couple a days so the bunkhouse is empty. Drop your bedrolls and kits on any bunks in the bunkhouse and come out to the bunkhouse porch. Breakfast is ready for you. There's plenty to eat and all the coffee you can drink. When you finish breakfast, put your dishes and utensils in the wash buckets you'll find next to the bunkhouse kitchen door. You'll have lunch and dinner here, too. Lunch will be ready at noon. Dinner is normally ready around sundown."

We all expressed our appreciation. John Fields smiled and nodded at us, turned toward the barn, and walked away. We did as suggested. We retrieved our bedrolls and kits from the buckboard, dropped them in the bunkhouse on empty bunks, and came out to the porch for breakfast, which was a feast, eggs, beans, steak, toast, and plenty of coffee.

After we'd eaten our fill and deposited our plates and utensils in the wash buckets, we went into the bunkhouse kitchen and thanked the cooks. We returned to the porch and sat waiting for instructions about what would come next.

We didn't have long to wait. Alexander stood at the head of the table and said, "I'm sure all of you are as tired as me. So, let's get a couple hours sleep and be back here at noon for lunch. After lunch, Bird and the Chiricahua will take us up the hill to look over the Bar CS. We'll be able to complete our plan after we've all seen how the Bar CS is laid out."

We all agreed with this and moved toward the bunkhouse door.

# 34

We began waking about noon. The first ones up purposely made enough noise to wake the others. We struggled out of our bedrolls and dressed. Lines quickly formed for the wash basins and the outhouse. Since I had slept, washed, and used the facilities here before, I made sure I was one of the first up and out.

I hurried to the bunkhouse kitchen for coffee and sat with my steaming cup at the end of the bench closest the kitchen waiting to be first in line for lunch, which was the usual feast. I loaded my plate, but not so much anyone after me would be left without. There was meat and potatoes and bread and butter, with enough coffee for triple our number. The cooks reminded us to be sure to return our plates and utensils to the appropriate buckets of hot water next to the side of the bunkhouse kitchen door.

As we ate, Alexander announced, "You've got 15 minutes to finish eatin', then saddle up. In 30 minutes we'll follow Bird and the Chiricahua up the hill to see the Bar CS and determine how best to round up the hands and keep the herd together. Your horses were fed and watered earlier this mornin' and watered again 'bout an hour ago. They're ready to go."

Everyone murmured in response and kept eating.

True to his word, 15 minutes passed and Alexander stood, deposited his dish and utensils in the water buckets and strode off toward the barn. We all followed, Lacy and I first, the others right behind us.

When we arrived at the barn, John Fields, Bird, and the Chiricahua were waiting for us. Our horses were tied to hitching rails in front of the barn. We curried our horses, checked and cleaned their feet, and tacked up as quickly as we could. When we were ready, we mounted, and sat our horses in an arc facing Alexander and the barn.

Alexander said, "From here on, hold your talkin' to a minimum. If you've anythin' to say, make sure it's a whisper and only if it's mighty important. Tomorrow's supposed to be a surprise for the Bar CS. We don't want 'em findin' out today that we're here. Any questions?"

No-one replied.

Alexander continued, "Good. Bird, Mangus, Mahko, and Gil-lee will lead us up the hill. Follow them single file. Leave extra space between you and the person in front of you. Loco and Taza left earlier and are stringin' a picket line 'bout 100 yards this side of the crest of the hill where we'll tie our horses. Loco and Taza will stay with the horses and keep 'em quiet while we're surveilling the Bar CS. Once you tie your horses and we're on foot, follow Bird, Mahko, Mangus, and Gil-lee up to the crest. We're aimin' for a pile of boulders. You can't miss 'em. There should be enough room either on the pile or around it for each of us to have a good view of the valley. Any questions?"

We looked Alexander and each other, but no-one replied. Bird spoke quietly to the Chiricahua, translating what Alexander said.

Alexander added, "And, lastly, these are what you should focus on: the size and shape of the valley; the location of the river and how it cuts the valley in half; the location of the stand of trees next to the river, the location of the main camp, the tents that make up the camp, the chuck wagon, the remuda, the ranches near the north edge of the valley, the hills that ring the valley, and where the hands are this mornin'. The hands will probably be in similar positions tomorrow mornin'. Any questions?"

We looked at Alexander and each other, but no-one had a question or anything to add. And, again, Bird spoke quietly to the Chiricahua, translating what Alexander said.

Alexander said, "OK. Bird, move 'em out. Take it slow and quiet. We've only got a mile to go so it shouldn't take long. Watch for Bar CS lookouts."

Bird and the Chiricahua turned their horses and rode around the back of the barn, through the gate, and started up the hill. We followed single file, first Alexander, Lacy, and me, then Knight, Every, Dyson, and Jackson. Bird set a slow pace and kept under or close to the trees so we'd be riding on pine needles to lessen the noise of our 11 horses. The risk was a horse stepping on and snapping a branch covered by pine needles on the ground. A snapping branch would sound like a gunshot in the quiet of the forest and could bring riders from the Bar CS to investigate.

We made it to the picket line without mishap. We dismounted and tied our horses, grouped up, and lit out single file behind Mahko, Mangus, and Gil-lee toward the boulder pile.

When we neared the boulders, Mahko, who was in the lead, held up his hand then pointed to the ground, indicating we should stop and get down, which we did. Mahko duck-walked to the boulders, silently climbed them, and grabbed a Bar CS lookout around the forehead from behind, pulled a knife from the top of his right mocasin, and slit the lookout's throat. He held the lookout off his feet until he stopped shaking and threw his lifeless body to the ground. Mangus and Gil-lee sprinted to the body, picked it up and carried it into the trees, and returned. Mahko motioned us to come.

We stood and advanced to the boulder pile. Alexander, Bird, and Knight climbed to the top. Lacy, Dyson, Jackson, and Every climbed to the boulders one level down from the top. The Chiricahua and I moved to positions on the ground from where we could see the whole valley, since we had been up here and seen the valley before.

While we were surveilling the valley, we kept in mind the things Alexander had told us to focus upon. I focused on the chuck wagon, fire pit, and mIn camp. I had told Knight and Every earlier to focus on the ranches at the north side of the valley next to the hills. I knew Bird and the Chiricahua would focus on the cattle and the others would focus on the locations of the Bar CS hands.

After about an hour, Mahko signaled for us to go back to the horses. We hurried through the trees to the picket line and grouped close to its southern end. Alexander and Knight walked off into the trees and reappeared in about 15 minutes.

Alexander said, "What a spectacular valley, perfect grass and plenty of water. They couldn't have asked for a better place to settle. Too bad they decided they could enlarge their herd at the expense of their neighbors."

Alexander stopped and waited for comments, but nobody spoke. Bird translated quietly for the Chiricahua.

Alexander continued, "Knight and I agreed on an approach to the Bar CS. Lacy, Dyson, and Jackson will cover the main camp.

Be prepared to face 12 or 13 men, Charles Stockett, the owner, Ed Vargas the foreman, eight or nine hands, and the cook and his helper. Emmett and I will cover night crew in the herd. I don't expect we'll run in to more'n two or three hands. Knight and Every will cover the three small ranches on the north side of the valley. You'll have three hands to deal with. Kill or capture 'em. No-one gets away. And, Bird and the Chiricahua will concentrate on keeping the herd together. With those assignments in mind, let's go back up to the boulder pile and take a fresh look into the valley. I expect we'll need less than an hour to get things firmly in our minds and decide how we do our assignments. Afterwards, we'll return to our horses and go back to the Runnin' Bird and get our timing down. Loco and Taza will take down the picket line and bring it back to the ranch. We don't want a Bar CS hand finding it during the night. Any questions?

We looked at Alexander and each other, but no-one had a question or anything to add. As before, Bird translated quietly for the Chiricahua.

We followed Mahko, Mangus, and Gil-lee to the crest of the hill and to the boulder pile. We formed into the groups that Alexander had assigned. Bird and Alexander climbed to the top level of the boulders. Knight and Every then Lacy, Dyson, Jackson, and I followed them up and stopped at the boulders slightly below the top, Knight and Every to their left and we four to their right. The Chiricahua stayed on the ground. Each of our groups focused on the objects of our assignments.

Alexander was right. It took close to an hour for each of us to decide how we and our group would do our assigned tasks. I could see the process in the faces, not all at the same time, but slowly one by one. First came an openness of taking in the panorama of the valley. Then came a look of deep thought, questioning, and focus. And lastly, a smile as the correct way to accomplish the task ahead was revealed.

Without speaking or coordinating our movements, we all climbed down the boulder pile together. We continued single file to the horses, checked our tack and tightened our cinches, mounted, and rode back to the Running Bird, single file as we had come up, Bird in the lead followed by Mahko, Mangus, Gillee and the rest of us. When we arrived at the Running Bird, we put up our horses and met on the bunkhouse porch.

Alexander said to us, "The cooks have lunch ready. After we eat, we'll discuss tomorrow."

We gratefully moved toward the bunkhouse kitchen to collect our meals. When we finished eating, we put our plates and utensils in the appropriate buckets of warm water by the entrance to the bunkhouse kitchen and returned to the tables and sat. Many of us were carrying freshened cups of hot coffee.

Alexander was standing at the head of the table. He addressed us, "Each group is to finalize its plan to accomplish its tasks. Groups should sit together apart from the others so you can concentrate of your tasks. Remember, you need to be in the Bar CS valley and located where you need to be before sunrise. That means you'll need to leave here at least two hours before sunrise. Knight, you and Every need to leave an hour earlier because the small ranches at the north side of the valley are that much further from here. Take as much time as you need to create workable plans. Once your individual plans are finished, we'll get back together and coordinate them into one. Now get in your groups and get to work. Remember, get to bed early, we'll be getting up at midnight."

Bird jumped up and added, "Dinner will be served here at sundown. Don't worry about your horses. They'll be fed and watered this afternoon and tonight."

# 35

Bird came into the bunkhouse just after midnight to awaken us. We were already up and dressing. We struggled outside and around to the bunkhouse kitchen, got coffee, and returned to the bunkhouse porch to drink our coffee and finish waking up. We were surprised to find the Chiricahua already on the bunkhouse porch waiting for us. One by one, as we finished our coffee, we picked up our rifles and headed to the barn to curry our horses, check their feet, and tack them up. The Chiricahua helped us tie rags around our horses' feet and around their snouts to keep them quiet.

We led our horses out of the barn, mounted, and when all or us were up and settled, we rode around to the back of the barn, through the gate, and up the hill to the east as quietly as possible. We stopped at the crest of the hill near the boulder pile to rest our horses and check for Bar CS lookouts. Seeing none, when our horses were again breathing normally, we rode down into the valley.

At the base of the hill, we split into three groups. It would have been four groups, but Knight and Every had left about an hour before us to the north and east following the edge of the valley toward the three small ranches. Their task was to capture or kill the Bar CS hands located there.

Lacy, Dyson, and Jackson rode east toward the main camp at the center of the valley. Their task was to capture or kill the Bar CS men at the tent camp, Charles Stockett, the owner of the Bar CS, his foreman, Ed Vargas, maybe eight or nine hands, and the cook and his helper.

Alexander and I rode east toward the stand of cottonwoods next to the river at the center of the valley. Our task was to find and capture or kill the Bar CS night crew. We weren't expecting more than two.

Bird and the Chiricahua followed several minutes behind Alexander and me toward the stand of cottonwoods. Their task was to take over night crew duty keeping the Bar CS herd calm, quiet, and in place after Alexander and I had killed or captured the Bar CS night crew.

# 36

Knight and Every nudged their horses into a jog trot, heading north and east toward the three ranches at the north side of the valley. The three ranches were between three and four miles distant, and because it was dark, they were being careful of uneven ground and holes. Knight thought it could take them nearly two hours to get to the ranches.

They rode just inside the pine trees bordering the edge of the valley. There, the ground was carpeted with needles, absorbing their horses' footfalls. They had to be extra careful about branches covered by the needles, since the noise from stepping on and snapping a branch would be as loud as a rifle shot.

They made it to the middle ranch and dismounted next to an empty corral. They tied their horses to the corral's top rail and stood listening to the night sounds, making sure horses in the next corral were quiet and they hadn't awakened the men in the cabin. When Knight was satisfied their arrival was undetected, they moved quietly to the cabin and circled it.

There was a door on the end of the cabin facing the corrals and a single window on the other end. The window was an oiled skin. Every stopped at the window and Knight continued around to the door, which was slightly ajar.

Knight burst through the door shouting, "COME AWAKE AND GET UP. STAND NEXT TO YOUR BUNKS WITH YOUR HANDS UP HOLDING AIR. COME AWAKE AND GET UP. STAND NEXT TO YOUR BUNKS WITH YOUR HANDS UP HOLDING AIR."

The men moved at the first set of commands and jumped out of their bunks. When the commands were repeated, the men stood straight up next to their bunks, hands in the air, scared to death.

Knight continued shouting, "I'm Rawlins Knight, Deputy Sheriff of Las Animas County, Colorado. You men are under arrest for rustlin'. Don't anyone move or I'll shoot."

Knight said more quietly, but loud enough for Every to hear, "Every, come on inside, gun drawn, with a good length of rope in hand."

When Every came in, Knight continued, "There's three of 'em. Tie 'em up together back-to-back and we'll have a talk with 'em."

Every said, "Move to the center of the room, sit on the floor, back-to-back."

The men did as they were told and waited. Every put a loop around them, pulled the rope tight, walked around them twice, and tied a solid knot in the rope.

Knight asked, "The punishment for rustlin' is hanging. We're gonna take you outside one at a time and strin' you up to a tree over yonder. You got anythin' to say for yourselves?"

The man closest to Knight said, "We didn't rustle nothin'. We arrived with the Bar CS herd and were sent here the next mornin' to raise vegetables, repair wagons, and build furniture. We don't know nothin' 'bout any rustlin'."

Knight answered, "The Bar CS has hundreds of cattle in its herd with brands from other ranches. Ranches near here. Those ranchers have complained to the local marshal and to me that they've recently lost over 500 head and we found 'em in the Bar CS herd. You work for the Bar CS, therefore you're as guilty of rustlin' as all the other Bar CS hands."

The same hand responded, crying and his voice breaking, "Please, deputy, it weren't us. We knew nothin' 'bout any rustlin'. Please let us go. We'll leave the county, leave the state, today. We'll go back to Texas and you'll never hear from us again."

Knight thought for a minute and answered, "OK, we'll let you go on one condition. You take what you can carry on your riding horses and one pack horse. Git your kits together, you've got ten minutes. We'll wait, see to it you're gone. Now move it."

# 37

Alexander rode over to Bird and said in a whisper, "You know what to do, keep the herd calm, quiet, and in place. Emmett and I'll find and eliminate the night crew before you scatter through the herd."

Bird replied, "Yes."

"Emmett and I are leavin' for the herd. You wait 15 minutes then follow us. Two of you go to the large herd west of the river. Two of you go to the large herd east of the river, and two of you go to the smaller herds north of the cottonwoods. You select who goes where. Questions?"

"No."

"Good. Translate for the Chiricahua."

Alexander motioned to me to come close. He turned from Bird to me and whispered, "We'll go to the cottonwoods near the center of the valley next to the river then split up. I'll go into the large herd west, you'll go into the large herd east of the river. When you find a rider kill or capture him quietly. Any noise and the action at the main camp will be jeopardized. If you have to kill someone, use your knife, don't shoot him. If you capture someone, tie his hands and feet and put a rag around his head after you stuff a rag or a rock in his mouth, then throw him over his horse, tie him on, and head back to the cottonwoods and wait for me. Questions?

"No."

Alexander waved at me indicating it was time to ride out and nodded at the others. We nudged our horses into a fast walk away from the group, heading east toward the cottonwoods.

When we were close to the river I smelled smoke and saw a small campfire burning near where the river cut through the cottonwoods. I motioned to Alexander and we dismounted, ground tied our horses, and silently approached the fire with Colts drawn. We stopped just short of the firelight and made sure of the number of hands at the fire, two, stretched out on the ground talking.

Alexander nodded at me and I nodded back, we were ready. Alexander jumped into the firelight, leveled his Colt at them, and said quietly, but commandingly, "DON'T MOVE! DON'T MAKE A SOUND! YOU MOVE OR MAKE A SOUND AND YOU'RE DEAD!"

Alexander gave them a moment for this to sink in and added, "SIT STRAIGHT UP! PUT YOUR HANDS TOGETHER IN FRONT OF YOU!"

To me, Alexander said, "Emmett, get some rope, tie their hands in front of 'em and leave each a long tail. We'll use the tails as leads when we bring 'em in."

I did as Alexander said and moved away from the two men.

Alexander said to them, "Your ranch has been rustlin' a few head at a time from the ten ranches around here. There must be more than 500 head in your herd that are carryin' other brands than the Bar CS. What do you know 'bout that?" Alexander waited, but neither of the Bar CS hands responded.

Alexander continued, "I'm sure you two were involved. Emmett and I'll take you to Deputy Knight and he'll take you to stand trial in Trinidad for rustlin'. You'll be strung up. Now, stand up, let's get you mounted and ride on over to your camp."

Just then, Bird and the Chiricahua rode into the firelight. They watched as we helped the the Bar CS hands mount, Alexander and I mounted, and we rode off toward the main camp.

# 38

Lacy, Dyson, and Jackson were the only ones left at the base of the hill at the west end of the valley. They nudged their horses into a jog trot and headed toward the main camp located close to the valley's center, on the east side of the river. When they arrived at the west side of the river, directly across from the main camp, they stopped, watched, and listened for any sounds or movement. Not hearing any, they quietly moved their horses into the river and slowly crossed.

They ground tied their horses and moved to the fire ring near the middle of the camp. Using hand signals they agreed upon a slight change of plan. First they placed several lengths of rope near the fire ring to tie up the Bar CS hands, if needed. Next they decided the two middle-sized tents housed the owner and foreman and the small tent next to the chuck wagon housed the cook and his helper. Lacy went to one of the two middle-sized tents to deal with its inhabitant, Dyson went to the other, and Jackson went to the small tent next to the chuck wagon. In a few minutes, Lacy and Dyson returned, each pushing a sleepy man in front of him. Jackson returned with two. As they expected, the men were Stockett, Vargas, and the cook and his helper. They tied three of them and sat them on the logs that circled the fire. They left the cook untied.

Jackson instructed the cook to bring the banked fire back to life. When the fire was happily burning and sparking, Jackson had the cook sit along side his helper and tied them securely together.

Jackson said to the cook, "I'm going to start ringing your triangle and you're gonna call the hands together for an early breakfast."

The cook nodded in response.

Jackson went over to the triangle and rang it good and loud. The cook yelled, "UP! UP! COME ON IN FOR BREAKFAST! HURRY, NOW!"

Lacy, Dyson, and Jackson moved outside of the light from the fire, drew their Colts, and waited.

The hands came fitfully awake, grumbling and cursing about being awakened so early, long before sunrise. They came to the crackling fire sloppily dressed, though five had strapped on their Colts and these men realized quickly that things were not as they seemed. They saw Stockett, Vargas, and the cook and his helper tied and sitting off to one side of the fire, and three strangers standing off to the other side with their Colts drawn.

The five Bar CS hands with Colts drew them, but they were too late. Lacy, Dyson, and Jackson were ready for them and cut them down along with two other Bar CS hands that had been unarmed, but had been caught in the crossfire. All together, seven Bar CS hands were down. The five with Colts hadn't gotten off a single shot.

Lacy asked Stockett, "Who were these seven hands?"

Stockett replied, "The two in back were two of my original crew who worked for me in Murphyville and come here on the drive. They were good men. It's too bad they're dead. The other five were gun hands, experienced trail drivers we hired in

Murphyville. They weren't the best of men, but they put in an honest day's work."

Lacy said, "No matter how they worked, they're dead and need to be buried. You'll see to digging the graves and bury 'em now while we're waiting for our friends."

Lacy untied one of the Bar CS hands and sent him for shovels. He returned with four. Lacy untied Stockett and Vargas and sent them with two other Bar CS hands to dig the graves.

# 39

While the dead Bar CS hands were being buried, Knight and Every arrived at the main camp from the small ranches at the north of the valley, and Alexander and I arrived soon thereafter from the herd with our night crew captives. We put our and the night crew's horses with the remuda and brought our captives to the campfire, putting them with the other captives and making sure they were tied securely.

Alexander said to the Lacy, "How 'bout untyin' the cook and his helper and have them fix us some breakfast. I'm really hungry and I bet ya'll are, too."

"Good idea," Lacy replied. "I'll see to it."

Lacy walked to where the cook and his helper were tied and cut their bindings. He said to them, "You're cut loose so you can make us breakfast. We expect you to stick around, not try to run off. If you try, you won't make it far. We'll be watching you closely."

As he walked off toward the chuck wagon, the cook replied over his shoulder, "Breakfast'll be ready in 'bout an hour. Don't worry 'bout us trying to run off, we won't."

When breakfast was ready, the cook's helper placed the hot food on the chuck wagon tailgate and called us to eat.

As we ate, Alexander said, "We need to rotate Bird and the Chiricahua in for breakfast, two at a time. Emmett and I'll go out to the herd. The first two we find, we'll send in to eat. When they finish, they'll return to the herd and send in another two. The last two will return to the herd and replace us. When

Emmett and I return, we have some business to discuss: getting the rustled cattle back to their owners; what to do with Stockett, Vargas, the cook and his helper, and the four remaining Bar CS hands; what to do with this valley; and, what to do with the Bar CS herd and equipment. Think about that until Emmett and I return."

Alexander and I collected our horses, and rode out. We found Bird and Mangus and sent them in for breakfast We did what they had been doing, slowly riding around talking soothingly to the cattle and sometimes singing or humming to them, a relaxing and fulfilling time. After a couple of hours, two Chiricahua came to us and signed that we could return to the main camp. We did.

When we arrive at the camp, we dismounted, put our horses with the remuda, and walked over to the camp fire. Lacy, Dyson, Jackson, Knight, and Every were sitting upwind of the campfire drinking coffee and talking. The Bar CS hands were still tied and sitting downwind of the campfire, looking uncomfortable from the ropes and the smoke. They looked angry. We got coffee and sat with our friends.

Alexander said, "Let's discuss what I mentioned before Emmett and I left. First, we got to return the rustled cattle to their owners. How should we do that?"

Knight answered, "The cattle are from ten ranches. We know which ranches they are by the brands, which cattle should go back where. It appears that cattle from each of the ranches have mostly stayed together and not mingled with cattle from other ranches. So, we try to keep the herd positioned as it is so the cattle don't mingle and we send riders to the ten ranches and have 'em send trail crews to come get 'em."

Alexander replied, "Good. I'll ask Bird to send a couple of hands out to the ranches and get that started tomorrow."

Alexander waited a minute for comments. None were made, so he continued, "We can either strin' up all the Bar CS hands here, now, or send 'em to Trinidad with Knight and Every for trial. Though, we could use the cook and his helper and some of the hands to handle the herd. What do you think we should do?"

I answered, "Lacy, Dyson, and Jackson killed the worst of 'em. I think the cook and his helper and the other hands shouldn't have to stand trial, they didn't initiate the rustlin' and they look as though they only went along with it to protect themselves. They should be offered jobs to remain with the Bar CS and its herd."

Alexander thought about what I said and responded, "Those are good ideas, but as of now there isn't a Bar CS for them to have jobs with."

I answered, "Alexander, you and I have been lawmen long enough. We should retire and become ranchers. You and I could take over the Bar CS. We could hire these men and the five Chiricahua, too. Knight and Every could take Stockett and Vargas back to Trinidad for trial."

Knight said, "Alexander, I agree with Emmett. There's no need for anyone but the top two to be brought in for trail."

Dyson and Jackson looked at each other said in unison, "We agree with Emmett."

Alexander thought a minute, staring off into the distance. He finally said, "Emmett, that'll work. It's 'bout time we gave up the law. You and I are getting a bit long in the tooth for all this. You make the offers to the Bar CS hands and the cook and his helper. I'll find Bird and ask him to talk with the Chiricahua. If they accept, Knight, Every, Dyson, Jackson, you, and I'll take Stockett and Vargas to the Runnin' Bird this afternoon, sleep there tonight, and continue on to Sunrise tomorrow. The Bar CS hands and the Chiricahua can stay and run this ranch until we get back."

I replied, "Alright, but we'll have to leave someone in charge. When I talk with the Bar CS hands 'bout staying, I'll think 'bout which one of them could be left in charge until we move here and talk to you 'bout it when you get back."

Alexander nodded and went for his horse to find Bird.

I sat for a spell putting my thoughts together about how to address the Bar CS hands and the cook and his helper then went to where they were tied. I said to them, "We've decided you six have a simple choice to make, join us or swing for rustlin'. If you join us, you'll agree to continue the jobs you've been doing for at least the next year and work with and for whomever we tell you. If you choose to leave, you'll go with Deputies Knight and Every to Trinidad and stand trial for rustlin', meanin' you'll probably swin' at the end of a rope. What'll it be?"

To a man, they enthusiastically said yes.

Alexander found Bird and said to him, "Bird, Emmett and I will be taking over the Bar CS. We'll keep the six remaining hands and the cook and his helper but we'll need more hands. Do you think the Chiricahua would stay and work for us?"

Bird replied, "I think all five would stay with you for a while, don't know how long, though probably at least a year. You really won't have any trouble talking with 'em, they all speak your language. They just didn't want you to know. Makho is their leader and he really knows cattle."

Alexander responded, "Good. Do you think Makho could handle being ranch foreman?"

Bird thought for a minute and answered, "I think he would be perfect, as long as he was accepted by the rest of the crew."

Alexander answered, "I can guaranty he won't have a problem with 'em."

Bird said, "Then I think you can count on all five of 'em staying with you. And, Claire and I would like you as neighbors. Have you considered bringing Ella and Jewel with you?"

Alexander smiled and said, "We'll have to see what develops with the women. Our plan is to leave the Chiricahua, the six Bar CS hands, and the cook and his helper with the herd. We'll take Stockett and Vargas to the Runnin' Bird this afternoon, spend the night, and continue on to Sunrise tomorrow morning. Is that OK?"

Bird answered, "Yes, and I'll go with you. I'll come back out here to the ranch every few days to check on things until you get back."

Alexander nodded and they left for the main camp. When they arrived, Alexander said to me, "The Chiricahua are in and Makho will be the new foreman. I'll go through Stockett's tent looking for guns, valuables, and papers, you go through Vargas' tent looking for the same. Afterwards, they can get some clothes and we'll leave for the Runnin' Bird."

# 40

Knight and Every stood guard with their Colts drawn and pointed at Stockett and Vargas as they picked out horses from the remuda, curried them, checked their feet, and tacked up. Every stepped back a pace, still holding his Colt pointed toward Stockett and Vargas as Knight held both their horses' reins while they mounted. Every holstered his Colt and tied their hands. Every mounted and Knight handed the reins to both horses to him and mounted. Every gave Knight the reins to Stockett's horse, keeping the reins to Vargas'.

With Knight and Every mounted and the prisoners secured, the rest of us mounted and the ten of us started off for the Running Bird. Bird led, followed by Alexander and Lacy riding abreast. Then came in single file, Knight and Stockett, Every and Vargas, and finally Dyson and Jackson riding abreast, and me at drag.

It was coming on to late afternoon and the shadows were getting long. It wouldn't be long before dark came upon us, so we hurried along as fast as we could, while still watching for holes, rocks, and fallen tree limbs. We couldn't afford to have anyone set afoot by an injured horse.

We arrived at the Running Bird just at sundown. John Fields must have heard us coming down the hill because he and several of his hands were waiting for us at the barn. The hands took our horses as we dismounted. We took our Winchesters and saddle bags off our saddles and let the hands lead our horses into the barn. I was carrying my eight-gauge.

John said, "We've been waiting for you. We cleared out the barn so there'd be room for your horses and we could properly care for 'em. My hands'll unsaddle, brush, water, and feed 'em. Your bedrolls are still on your bunks. Get cleaned up and come to dinner on the bunkhouse porch as quickly as you can. Dinner's ready. You'll also have breakfast there tomorrow mornin'. I assume you'll be leaving after that."

Alexander answered, "Yes, John. We'll be out of here tomorrow after breakfast."

Knight said to Bird, "After we eat, you got a secure place to put Stockett and Vargas or should we tie 'em to bunks?"

Bird replied with a smile, "You'll have to tie 'em. We don't have a jail."

We ate a quiet diner and went to bed early. Even Stockett and Vargas were quiet and didn't complain about being tied to their bunks. All of us were tired and emotionally drained from the excitement of the day. But, we were happy we'd all returned unhurt, though we weren't the least bit upset about five of the Bar CS hands we'd killed.

We rose early the next morning, just at sunrise. We washed, changed clothes, and made ready for breakfast, which was a feast as usual. We packed our bedrolls and kits and straggled to the barn with them to get ready to leave. We put our bedrolls and kits on the buckboard and readied our horses. John Fields had one of his hands hitch the horse to the buckboard and tie its load down.

We said goodbye to Bird, Claire, and John Fields and left the Running Bird through the main gait. After warming up our horses for about ten minutes at a good flat walk, we broke into a jog trot to eat up the distance, stopping every so often to let them blow, drink, and get a mouthful or two of grass. We didn't dismount. We were hurrying so Knight and Every and their prisoners and Dyson and Jackson would make the morning train, but we knew the morning train would probably be late and we needn't have hurried.

We rode straight to the train station and found we had arrived before the train. Knight purchased tickets to Trinidad for himself, Every, Stockett, and Vargas and space in the stock car for their four horses. Dyson and Jackson purchased tickets to Penance for themselves and space in the stock car for their two horses. Dyson and Jackson would load their horses last as they would be leaving the train first. The train was late, but should arrive soon. There wasn't reason for us to wait with them, so we said our farewells.

Alexander, Lacy, and I mounted up and rode to the livery to put up our horses. Then we walked to City Hall and the marshal's office. No-one was waiting for us and neither were there any messages, so we slowly walked the town doing our rounds. It was quiet, few people were on the street, and only a few in the saloons. We returned to City Hall and sat out front on the boardwalk.

Alexander said, "Been thinkin' of our ranch. Doesn't seem right to call it the Bar CS. We need a new name. One that suits us."

Lacy and I thought for the proper amount of time a question like that deserved.

Lacy answered first, "The name should be a combination of your two names or somethin' that brings your names to mind."

Alexander and I thought for the proper amount of time that statement deserved.

I responded, "We could call it the Bar GM.  That combines our names."

We three thought for another proper amount of time.

Alexander said, "Could call it the Double Bar G8.  Be easier to run that over Bar CS, though the '8' don't mean nothin'."

Lacy and I thought about that for the proper amount of time then nodded our approval.

I said, "We gotta drink on that."

I went into the marshal's office and returned with a bottle of whisky and three glasses.  I filled our glasses and said to Alexander, "Here's to a new beginnin'."

We raised our glasses and each took a solid swallow of whiskey.  I continued looking Alexander straight in the eye, "Since we're gonna become ranchers and settle down, we should take Ella and Jewel to live with us on the Double Bar G8.  They could help us establish the ranch, build our houses, and create new lives.  We should marry 'em and make 'em respectable."

Alexander sat upright like my words had slapped across the face.  He sat stone still.  Neither Lacy nor I dared move or say a word.  We waited.

Finally Alexander seemed to relax and smile.  He said, "Good idea, but we'll have to wait and see what develops."

# Appendix

## CHARACTERS

| Characters | Description |
| --- | --- |
| Aldus White | Previous Police Chief of Sunrise, CO |
| Alexander Gadson | Marshal of Sunrise, CO |
| Bob | Bar CS scout |
| Charles Stockett | Bar CS owner |
| Claire Knowles | Running Bird ranch co-owner |
| Clay McCans | Chicago House Saloon and Hotel bartender |
| Dyson Lewis | Marshal in Penance, Colorado |
| Ed Vargas | Bar CS ranch foreman |
| Emmett Masters | Deputy Marshal Sunrise, Colorado |
| General Halsey Love | Union General and Sleeping L ranch owner |
| George Every | Deputy Sheriff Las Animas County, Colorado |
| Gerald Kroutsch | Bellas bartender and swamper |
| Gregory Jackson | Marshal in Penance, Colorado |
| Gil-lee | Chiricahua, one of five |
| Harold | Bar CS scout |
| Jay Rolf | Long X ranch foreman |
| Jewel Marion | Whore at Chicago House Saloon and Hotel, girl friend of Emmett Masters |
| Jim Slatter | Open A ranch foreman |
| John Fields | Running Bird ranch foreman |
| Jon | Bar CS scout |
| José | Mexican houseboy at the Sleeping L |

| Characters | Description |
| --- | --- |
| | Ranch (Running Bid Ranch) |
| Kati Madri | Whore at Bellas |
| Lacy Burnham | Deputy Marshal Sunrise, Colorado |
| Lefty | Bar CS scout |
| Loco | Chiricahua, one of five |
| Lowell Williams | Silver Chalet Saloon owner |
| Mahko | Chiricahua, one of five |
| Mangus | Chiricahua, leader of five |
| Pajarito (Bird) Corre | Running Bird ranch co-owner |
| Rawlins Knight | Deputy Sheriff Las Animas County |
| Sabrina White | Aldus White's widow, whore, and co-owner of Bellas |
| Sebastian Gomez | Owner of the Café Madrid |
| Snake | Bar CS scout |
| Stella (Ella) Penn | Alexander Gadson's ex-girlfriend, whore, and co-owner of Bellas |
| Taza | Chiricahua, one of five |
| Ward Layne | Chicago House Saloon and Hotel owner |

# LOCATIONS – CITIES

| Cities | Description |
| --- | --- |
| CO, Penance | Small town located northwest of Sunrise and southeast of Trinidad |
| CO, Sunrise | Small town located southeast of Penance |
| CO, Trinidad | County Seat of Las Animas County located northwest of Penance |
| TX, Marfa | West Texas, next railroad stop west of Murphyville |
| TX, Murphyville | West Texas, original location of the Bar CS ranch, mid-way between Marfa and Sanderson |
| TX, Sanderson | West Texas, next railroad stop east of Murphyville |

# LOCATIONS – BUSINESSES AND OTHERS

| Businesses and Others | Description |
| --- | --- |
| Bellas | Gentlemen's club in Sunrise, co-owned by Stella (Ella) Penn and Sabrina White |
| Café Madrid | Only stand alone restaurant in Sunrise |
| Chicago House Saloon and Hotel | Saloon and hotel in Sunrise owned by Ward Layne |
| City Commission | Commission that oversees town building and projects |
| City Hall | Sunrise City Hall built upon the insistence of Aldus White when he was preparing to run for mayor |
| Mercantile | Store in Sunrise, CO |
| New Marshal's Office | Located in the new Sunrise City Hall |
| Old Marshal's Office | Located across the street from the Chicago House Saloon and Hotel in Sunrise, has a three-cell jail |
| Silver Chalet Saloon | Saloon in Sunrise owned by Lowell Williams |
| Sweets Café | Restaurant in Trinidad |

# RANCHES

| Ranch Name | Brand | Description |
|---|---|---|
| Bar CS | <u>CS</u> | Ranch east of the Running Bird, moved from Murphyville, TX |
| Bar M | A̶A̶ | Ranch north of the Running Bird |
| Circle R | Ⓡ | Ranch west of the Running Bird |
| Double Bar G8 | <u>G8</u> | Bar CS ranch renamed the Double Bar G8 |
| Flying O | -O- | Ranch south of the Running Bird |
| Hashknife | ⊖ | Ranch west of the Running Bird |
| Long X | ✕ | Ranch north of the Running Bird |
| N Bar N | N—N | Ranch south of the Running Bird |
| Open A | ∧ | Ranch north of the Running Bird |
| Rafter J | ↥ | Ranch west of the Running Bird |
| Running Bird | ⤙ | Sleeping L Ranch given to Bird Corre and Claire Knowles by Alexander Gadson and renamed the Running Bird |
| Running W | ᨑ | Ranch north of the Running Bird |
| Sleeping L | ⅂ | General Halsey Love Ranch given to Alexander Gadson after the death of General Love |

# Acknowledgements

I want to acknowledge four people who helped me write this book. Their help was invaluable and I deeply appreciate their assistance.

## KATHLEEN P. KATZ

Mrs. Katz is my bride of 50 years. She has given me encouragement, intellectual stimulation, and loving kindness throughout this and many other endeavors. She is an accomplished horsewoman and has been my riding and camping companion for most of my life. She has taught me most of what I know about riding and how to care for and treat my horses. She rides Arabs and I ride Tennessee Walking Horses. She says I ride this breed of horse because I don't really want to know how to ride. Several parts of this story were based on her ideas, thank you.

## LOUIS ROBINSON

I am privileged to have Mr. Robinson and his wonderful wife as friends. Mr. Robinson is an accomplished writer who has published several books and is the retired Managing Editor of *Ebony Magazine*. Mr. Robinson provided timely and poignant critiques that were a tremendous help, thank you.

## HEATHER M. SMITH

Ms Smith, my daughter, is the Managing Editor of *Drumhead Magazine*. She lives and works in Manhattan, that's New York City. Ms Smith was a fearless critic who attacked every page for spelling, punctuation, consistency, and story line.  It pays to have a professional in the family, thank you.

### ROBERT M. COBB

Mr. Cobb has been my friend and riding and camping companion for more than 35 years.  We have ridden the mountains and deserts all over the western part of the United States, including Kennedy Meadows, Beach Meadows, and Wild Horse in the California High Sierras, Canyon de Chilly National Monument in Arizona, Point Reyes National Seashore in California, Big Bend National Park in Texas, and ridden together more than 150 miles crossing Death Valley National Park in California 11 times from 1976 through 2008.  He has taught me significant things about riding the back country and how to treat my horses, thank you.

### PETER CHARLTON

I purchased a map entitled "The Lonesome Dove Trail, The Comanche Moon Wars, The Great Cattle Trails" from Mr. Charlton through Amazon.com.  Mr. Charlton was kind enough to permit me to use a portion of his map on the cover of this book.  Please visit Mr. Charlton's website, www.lectricbooks.com.

### TEXAS ALMANAC

The Texas Almanac website (www.texasalmanac.com), created and maintained by the Texas State Historical Association, contains a wonderful article entitled *Cattle Drives Started in Earnest After the Civil War*.  This article provides excellent historical information.  The Texas Almanac was kind enough to permit me to use materials from its website in this book.

## FORT TUMBLEWEED

The Fort Tumbleweed website (www.forttumbleweed.net), created and maintained by Leonard and Lynda Kubiak, contains an excellent article entitled *True Texas Tales: History of Cowboys and Trail Drives in Early-Day Texas*. This article provides excellent historical information. Mr. Kubiak was kind enough to permit me to use materials from his website in this book.

# About the Author

Howard Katz was born in Chicago, Illinois, and moved with his parents to Los Angeles, California, as an infant. He went to public school in Southern California, graduating from Burbank High School. He graduated from San Fernando Valley State College (now known as California State University Northridge) with a dual major in History and Anthropology. He later did graduate work in Anthropology at Cornell University.

Howard began working for IBM in 1963 and retired after 30 years in 1993. While with IBM, Howard worked as a Systems Engineer, Salesman, Programmer, and Senior Staff Member. After leaving IBM, Howard worked as a Project Director for an information technology consulting company in Dallas, Texas, a Consulting Practice Manager for Oracle Corporation, and as Director of Club Application Development for 24 Hour Fitness.

Howard's jobs in information technology allowed him and his family to travel extensively throughout the United States, Canada, the Caribbean, Europe, and Asia. Howard and his wife and family lived a total of 14 years abroad in Caracas, Venezuela, several locations in Europe, and Tokyo, Japan.

In 2001, Howard left information technology to teach high school in the Perris Union High School District in Perris, California. He retired from teaching in 2008.

Howard and his wife and family have had horses for more than 40 years. They have camped with their horses and ridden in California, Nevada, New Mexico, Texas, and Oklahoma. They have ridden 140 miles across Death Valley, California, 11 times. While living 13 years in Dallas, Texas, Howard and his wife and family, took their horses to Big Bend National Park and camped and rode for two weeks in the park every winter. Howard has competed successfully with his horses in 25 and 50 mile endurance races. Howard rides a Tennessee Walking Horse and his wife rides an Arab.

www.ingramcontent.com/pod-product-compliance
Lightning Source LLC
Chambersburg PA
CBHW070101260626
47160CB00004B/1278